MAGICNET

JOHN DeCHANCIE

An AvoNova Book

William Morrow and Company, Inc.
New York

AVON BOOKS
A division of
The Hearst Corporation
1350 Avenue of the Americas
New York, New York 10019

Library of Congress Cataloging in Publication Data:

DeChancie, John.
    Magicnet / John DeChancie.
        p.   cm.
I.   Title
PS3554.E1785M3 1993   93-14429
813'.54—dc20   CIP

First Morrow/AvoNova Printing: December 1993

*This one is for you, Ray;
and, yes, I wish I'd done it
sooner, but you know me.
Rest easy, my friend.*

In Memoriam

Ramon Kenneth May

1946-1991

*Special thanks to John Douglas, my editor;
and to Susan and Harlan Ellison,
without whose assistance, cooperation, and hospitality
at least one chapter of this book would be blank pages.*

1

I AWAIT THE DIVINE THUNDER, HERALD OF
of the new age, which, I guess, by odious rictus of
recalculation brings us back to the beginning of this
tale:

Sunday night.

A preternatural quiet, nothing happening. I think
of Sunday evening as a transitional period, a hushed
pause between the end of one week and the beginning
of another. I'm always reminded of something out of
Norse mythology: the Ginnungagap, the timeless epoch
of nothingness between the cycles of existence, similar
in concept to the *ricorso* of Vico's cyclical history, which
Joyce puts to convoluted use in *Finnegans Wake*.

On that particular Sunday evening, when all this
recent business started, I was home, reading. My house
stood at the edge of the campus, a convenient walk away
from the buildings where I taught my classes. It was also
a leisurely stroll to the post office, to a few of the town's
best restaurants, and to the still-operating single-screen
"nabe" movie house, which most autoless students pa-
tronized, the six-screen mall complex being miles away,
near the Interstate. The house was also not far from
some other conveniences, including the supermarket

where I did my grocery shopping. In short, it was a nice location, for all that the house was small and old and borderline-ramshackle. I don't mean to imply that the place was structurally unsound. To paraphrase the laconic engineer in Mr. *Blandings Builds His Dream House*—as he sizes up the old colonial horror that Cary Grant and Myrna Loy want to buy—the sills were shot but the beams were still good, or vice versa; but not both, in which case I would have torn it down and rebuilt on the property. (I could have afforded it even on my assistant professor's salary, as the house was paid off and I had supplemental income from a trust fund; but I digress.)

That March night was especially quiet and unusually mild. Earlier, around seven, Sharon and I had eaten pasta primavera at Mineo's, a little place right off campus. We had kissed good-night a block away from my house; she had a paper to finish and I an honors seminar to prepare for. Sharon was working on her master's; a rabid medievalist, she was taking a course in Scots poetry and was enthused to the point of wanting to do her thesis on it. So, it was a fond kiss, then we severed. I sent her off into the almost-spring tenderness of the night, and went home.

In my study, a little alcove off the living room, I read a little, took some notes, and keyed them into the CLASSNOTES directory on my computer's hard disk. I printed out a crib sheet, and was done as far as preparing how I wanted to steer the discussion tomorrow in my seminar on Romantic English poetry. Then I settled down in the living room with Keats's "The Fall of Hyperion." Impelled by yet another obscure classical allusion that needed more explication than the *Norton Anthology* supplied (with Byron, Keats, and

Shelley, you never seem to run out of classical allusions), I dipped into Bulfinch and promptly got lost, wandering off the Hellenic trail into the Celtic thicket of the *Mabinogion*.

The phone rang.

"Hello," I said, eyes and attention still on the exploits of Peredur, son of Evrawc.

"Skye?"

I recognized the voice, and there was a nervous edge in it that was immediately perceptible. "Hi, Grant. What's up? Anything wrong?"

"Yeah, maybe a lot. Look, I don't know how much time I have, but I'm in a shitload of trouble."

I put down Bulfinch. "Grant, what is it?"

"Don't have time to explain. I'm getting ready to take off, leave town for a while. I'm not going to say where I'm going or even what mode of transportation I'm going to use. Suffice it to say that I'm getting the fuck out of here, and quick."

"That bad?"

"Yeah, that bad. Look, I mailed something to you. A package. Don't open it unless—okay, this is going to sound dramatic—but don't open it unless something happens to me. Got that?"

"You mailed a package? What's in it? And what leads you to think that something might happen to you?"

"Skye, I don't have time to explain. Believe me, explaining would be a major problem even if I had the time. I've got into some strange business lately . . . weird. You wouldn't believe it. Anyway, look, I have to run—oh, shit."

There was silence on the other end of the line.

"Grant?"

Grant's voice came in a frightened whisper. "Something's in the backyard. Christ. Skye, listen—"

"Grant, what the hell's wrong?"

"Call the cops. Shit, it's too late. Skye, don't tell anyone about the stuff I sent you. *Not even the cops! You hear?*"

"Grant, tell me what's going on!"

"I can't. Oh, my God. *No!*

"Grant?" I heard the phone thunk, then heard Grant yell. There came a shattering of glass, crashing sounds, another piteous yell from Grant, sounds of struggle . . .

I was on my feet yelling into the phone, my heart spasming. More crashing, then silence.

"Grant?"

Silence continued for a few moments. Then I continued my ear-witnessing as someone began moving about Grant's apartment, making a racket. I heard the crash of overturning furniture and the shattering of glass. Dazed, I stood there longer than I should have, then finally found the presence of mind to push the little tab on the cheap, generic Pacific Rim telephone that should have broken the connection, but didn't. I tried it again, in vain.

Vagaries of the local phone company: in this particular small-town subsystem you could not get a dial tone if you hung up on somebody and they stayed on the line, a boon to obscene phone callers and nuisance telemarketing solicitors. Why this was so was anybody's guess, but it was so. I couldn't get a dial tone to punch in a call to the police, and was forced to continue listening helplessly to the sounds of the brutal, systematic sacking of Grant's apartment.

At length the commotion stopped. Silence, except for the tread of feet. Then, somebody picked up the phone and listened, breathing into the mouthpiece.

The sound was like a wind off a malarial swamp. There was something septic about it; somehow I smelled noxious fumes as the breath whistled hot against my ear.

I stood there, ice crystals forming around my heart. Time dragged. I couldn't seem to detach the phone from the side of my head.

Finally, there came a metallic clunk again, as of a phone being dropped, and the sound of heavy footsteps receding.

I hung up and ran to the door, snagging my brown leather World War II Army Air Force jacket en route.

A big Gothic moon was just edging out from behind a cloud as I ran through sleepy college-town shadows. Cracked sidewalks at my athletic-shoed feet, bare maples overhead, yellow lighted windows at either hand. I ran as fast as I could, my thirty-six-year-old lungs, carcinogenically abused for twenty of those thirty-six, for some reason not protesting as I had thought they would. I never run. I make it a point to avoid trendy behavior (except for having quit smoking, something my lungs had put their metaphorical foot down about) even when such contrariness runs counter to ancient wisdom. After all, there's nothing wrong with exercise; moderately indulged in, it can even be salubrious. But it so happens I'm of the opinion that most people, middle-aged men especially, attired in sweats or, worse, in Yuppie track outfits (head- and/or wristbands really get to me), dutifully puffing along in slavish obedience to the dictates of the current doyen of the health gurus, look—to put it bluntly—like assholes. (That I might be laughing all the way to the cardiac unit doesn't seem to alter this perception.)

But now I ran. Sharon's apartment house was about

ten blocks away, and I covered half the distance in about two minutes. I had to slow to a jog for the rest of the way, but arrived in front of Sharon's building still breathing regularly and in what for me was record time. Adrenaline can do wonders.

I leaped up the steps, entered the building, bounded up a flight, and pounded on her door. It took her a while to bestir herself. I pounded again.

The door opened and I barged in.

"Skye! What—?"

"Grant's in trouble. Where's the phone?"

"In my bedroom. Skye, what's the matter?"

"I don't know, but something's happened out there and it didn't sound good." I went into her small bedroom.

Sitting on her double bed, I dialed 9-1-1.

"Emergency Service." A woman's voice.

"Yes, I want to report a possible break-in and assault."

"What's your name and address, sir?"

"It didn't happen at my place. I heard it over the phone. I was talking to a friend and I heard crashing, someone breaking in, and he screamed, and—"

"Sir, you say you heard this on the phone?"

"Yes, I was talking to my friend, and I heard someone break in . . . and something happened. I don't know what, but I think my friend may be hurt."

"Where does your friend live, sir?"

I had already snapped my fingers imperiously at Sharon, whispering "Phone book!" I didn't know Grant's address. I knew where he lived, out in the sticks, could even get there, but didn't know what municipality it was. There were several outlying townships surrounding College Green.

"Sir? We need an address."

Sharon handed me the book just as I remembered that Grant's number was unlisted.

"Look, I don't know exactly what the street address is, but it's a house on Route 218 somewhere either in Clinton Township or Tuscarora Township, somewhere out there."

"Sir, that's going to be a little hard to find."

"Shit! I know. Goddamn it!"

"Sir, just remain calm," she said with professional smoothness.

"Right." She was right, of course. "Look, it's a little house on the outskirts of one of those little hamlets out there . . . I can't remember. Westonville! Yeah, I think that's it." Sharon nodded, remembering, too.

"Westonville?"

"Yeah, I think. He lives just on the edge of town."

"What is this person's name, sir?"

"Grant Barrington. It's a white clapboard house with an overgrown front yard, and there should be an old blue Volvo parked in the dirt driveway."

"What is your name and address, sir?"

"King. Schuyler King, 367 South Barnard Street, College Green."

"Would you spell that first name, please?"

"No time! Please, I'm telling you something happened to him. He may be badly hurt."

"We'll rush an ambulance right there, sir. Don't worry, and please stay calm."

"I'm sorry, yes, right. Please hurry."

Exhaling, I put the phone down. Sharon looked appalled.

"My God, Skye, what happened?"

"I don't know. As Grant and I were talking, somebody broke into his house and did something to him. Whatever it was, it sounded awful. I heard Grant scream. For all I know he could be dead. I have to get out there. Can you drive me?"

"Sure. Skye, do you really think . . . ?"

"I don't know what to think. Let's go."

2

SHARON'S CAR, A BATTERED FORD ESCORT, WAS parked on the street. We got in, she turned the key, and the starter motor groaned complainingly. The car's battery was old and needed replacing. The engine wheezed, and my anxiety began to spike. Then the thing finally started. I heaved a sigh of semirelief as I snapped on the seat belt.

Grant and I went back a long way. Grant's career as a campus hanger-on and perpetual student went back even farther. He was in his late forties, a veteran of the anti–Vietnam War movement of the sixties and early seventies. I was a freshman in 1971 and met him at an antiwar "teach-in." The war was soon to end, but Grant had been active in the peace movement even before the war escalated. I was as antiwar as the next Fabian socialist, but by the end of the 1970s I had reservations about certain positions to the extreme left. I was a pacifist at least in theory, and I found it problematical to cast a blanket condemnation over warfare yet give tacit approval and sometimes active support to various wars of "national liberation," each one more vicious and destructive than the last, all of which to date have yielded nothing but monstrous regimes whose enormities are well-documented. The homicidal demoniacs of the

Pol Pot epoch in Cambodia dealt the coup de grace to my waning progressivism, and a gnawing sense of *mauvaise foi* regarding pacifism—I had to face the fact that I was not a pacifist in practice—eventually prompted my ideological weaning from the extreme left. This might need some explication. Although my longtime belief in the inevitability and desirability of socialism lies in ruins, I have not become a paleoconservative, and will have no truck with fundamentalists. I regard as nonsense the view that a retreat from the left means motion toward prejudice, belligerence and pinch-heartedness. Don't tell anyone, but an old died-in-the-corduroy Bohemian like me can be anything *but* a conservative. That I am sometimes taken for one is but a telltale of how far the Zeitgeist has drifted toward the gonzo green anarchist, earth-and-animals-first, neo-Bakuninist fringe of the spectrum; and all this after the fall of the Soviet Union.

However, by the time I returned to my undergraduate alma mater with a Ph. D., Ronald Reagan was in the White House, the trend was to the right, and I had lost contact with most of my leftist friends, except Grant. He was still around and still leading the sort of aging-hippie life that seemed to fit him like an old suit.

Not that he didn't work. He was a computer programmer and a good one; he had been one back in antebellum days before personal computers, before everyone and his second cousin fiddled with computers (it seems that way sometimes), the beginning of his career dating to the cybernetic Paleozoic of IBM cards and keypunch machines. He now worked for a software development firm, the exact nature of whose products I was not familiar with. I was not a computer person. I owned a computer and used it, but aside from knowing how to run a word processor and a few utility programs, I knew next to nothing about programming, much less about the arcane mysteries of "systems," whatever that (or they) may be.

For all his early activism, Grant was never really political. As was true for any number of his generation, his had been a revolution more of style than of substance. Perhaps that was why we were still friends. Grant found my born-again capitalist views quaint, somewhat laughable, but not really pernicious, at least not enough to warrant breaking off the friendship. In fact, I had suspected recently that his views were changing as well, but in which direction they were tending I didn't know.

All of this came back to me as we raced through the almost-spring night, passing through the outskirts of town and out into the rural quietude of College Green's environs. The university was the main industry in the area, agriculture running a distant second. Most local farmers had to work at least part-time at a regular job that lay at the end of a long commute. Grant's employer was almost sixty miles away, but Grant had never moved, preferring to keep in touch with university life. Besides, he did a lot of work at home, via modem.

"What could have happened?" Sharon wondered. "A burglar, do you think?"

I shrugged. "Possibly," I said, remembering all too well that fetid breath in my ear. That the mere sound of it could have conveyed a sense of overwhelming malevolence was as puzzling as it had been frightening.

"Is he in any kind of trouble?" Sharon asked.

"For instance?"

Sharon ran a hand through her curly and unfashionably long hair. "I don't know. Does he do drugs?"

11

Grant, as far as I knew, hadn't "done" (strange how sixties argot lingers) drugs since the early seventies, and even then had never been a real druggie. A little pot, maybe LSD once (though I didn't know that for sure), possibly an early dalliance with cocaine, but recently Grant had come down hard against drug use, especially as regards "crack" cocaine. He had even sworn off alcohol.

"No, I don't think so. If he does, he keeps it quiet."

"Then it must have been a break-in," Sharon said.

For some reason I decided to delay telling her about Grant's allowing that he was indeed in a great deal of unspecified trouble.

We drove on into the dark countryside, passing an occasional house. When we hit 218 Sharon didn't know which way to turn, and I thought it was left, though I hadn't been out Grant's way in a while—I didn't own a car (one of the reasons for my continued solvency on an assistant professor's salary). It turned out I was right, and we rolled through sleepy Westonville, a collection of roadside houses cut by one cross street. We passed the last house and moved on into more rural repose.

It was in the midst of this dark nothingness that Grant's house stood. It was a small bungalow with no garage, a toolshed in the back. The long front yard, edged by a gravel drive, was high with hay and thick with weeds. Grant owned the place, and why he'd bought it was anybody's guess. The price had been right, I suppose. He had fixed it up some, but it still had a seedy look to it and badly wanted a coat of paint. The house was completely dark, looking as though no one were home, and I began to get the strangely disembodied feeling that I was the victim of a cruelly elaborate practical joke.

Grant's blue Volvo was in the drive, parked in its usual spot. We pulled up behind it and Sharon stopped the Escort's motor. A hush fell. This was a rare moment: one in which I regretted not owning a gun.

"Do you think they could still be around?" Sharon asked.

"I don't know," I said. "The cops sure are taking their time getting here."

"Yeah. Maybe we better wait."

"You stay here. I'm going to take a look."

She pressed my hand. "Skye, be careful."

"I will." I took a look at the house. "You have a flashlight?"

"I think." Sharon rummaged among the debris in a plastic tray between the bucket seats. She came up with something thin and small and handed it to me: a penlight.

"This is all I have," she said apologetically.

I pressed the clip and sent a weak beam of light against the floorboards.

"It'll have to do," I said.

I got out and approached the house. Crossing the lawn and tripping over obstructions half-seen in the dim beam of the penlight—a broken lawn chair, something deformed and soft (a deflated soccer ball?)—I muttered imprecations against Grant's habitual sloppiness. Uninjured, I reached the front door, which was locked. I rang the bell, hoping the assailant would take his cue and get the hell out. Nothing stirred in the house.

I went around the side. In the back I stopped beside the vacuum-treated-lumber deck Grant had recently built himself. The sliding glass door, which he'd installed with the deck, was smashed. The room inside was dark.

I checked the backyard. Moonlight revealed nothing but a few trees, the toolshed, and one of the more expensive self-orienting satellite dishes, a white high-tech flower upturned to a dark sky. For Grant, the latest and best technology was not a luxury. He had to have it. Lawn chairs and other trivialities he was content to get from cut-rate department stores.

I hopped over the deck's railing, went to the smashed door, and looked in, playing the penlight's beam around the room.

The place was a shambles. The components of several computers lay smashed on the floor. There was debris all over, shelves cleared of their hundreds of books, the contents of drawers strewn across the room; furniture upset; the entire kitchen—Grant had removed a wall to make an open floor plan—reduced to rubble. Computer diskettes lay scattered like dark leaves all over the house.

I saw a pair of legs sticking out from behind the couch. Edging carefully through the jagged hole in the sliding door, I went in.

And there he was. Grant. He lay on his back, eyes rounded in a final terror, mouth agape, his throat laid open like a watermelon. It looked as though something had taken a bite out of him. Blood pooled beside him, staining the blue-gray carpet darkly.

I don't know how long I stared at Grant's body. Presently I wrenched my gaze from it and slumped to the couch, trying to stop my nerves from jangling. I felt like throwing up. I had never seen anyone murdered before, let alone a close friend.

At length, I gathered together what was left of my nerve and got up. I tried a light switch. Nothing. There was no overhead fixture, and all the lamps were smashed.

I stumbled around the room trying to find a source of illumination, to no avail.

The door to the single bedroom was closed. I stood before it, listening. I heard nothing. Hoping that the bedroom had been left unmolested and that there was a usable lamp and a telephone in there, I turned the fake-brass knob and opened the door.

I didn't see much—just a tall shape in the almost negligible penlight beam, but what there was of it froze my heart. Red eyes glowed at me. Below them was a snoutful of sharply glinting teeth, and from it came something like a growl, half-human and monstrous, a full-throated version of what I had heard over the phone.

I leaped back and slammed the door, but it wouldn't close. The creature's taloned claws hung in front of my face, and I yelled and dropped to my knees, yanking against the doorknob. The creature yowled. The knob slipped out of my hands and I fell backward. I rolled, got up and tried to run, but tripped and fell, entangled in electrical cords and newspapers. I lost the penlight.

The thing, a hideous outline against the shadows, burst out of the bedroom and came at me. I thrashed loose and rolled away, coming up painfully against an overturned wooden chair. I grabbed it and rose, thrusting it out in classic beast-taming fashion. The creature swiped and tore splinters from the chair. I backstepped, fending the thing off. The sounds it made were horrible. It wanted me, and would not stop till it had me. I tripped over something, staggered, but kept on my feet, retreating steadily into the living room. The creature kept advancing, snarling and slavering, its claws quickly reducing the chair to kindling.

The thing lunged at me. I retreated and fell over something, ending up on the living room rug facedown, wedged between the couch and a leather ottoman.

My leg was caught and I struggled. The creature stopped and seemed to listen. Then it brought its gaze around to me again. It snarled once more. The sound was inhuman yet intelligent. I sensed its frustration, its unslaked blood lust.

Suddenly the creature—whatever it was—turned and left.

Before long, smudges of red light began to chase each other on the ceiling, and I looked at them blankly a moment before realizing that the police must have arrived. The doorbell rang.

I freed myself and rose. Groping, I found a light switch, and this time something was connected. Against the far wall, a lamp lying on its side lighted up.

The doorbell rang again. I opened the front door. A state trooper, hand on his revolver, stood holding the screen door open.

"Any trouble here?" the trooper asked.

"Plenty," I said. "My friend is dead. In there."

Warily, the trooper entered.

Sharon came in after him and I took her in my arms.

"Is he—?"

I nodded.

"Oh, my God! Skye, what *happened?* I heard all this noise!"

"Something attacked me. Whatever it was, it killed Grant."

We hugged each other until one of the cops came back into the front room. Flashlights lighted up the back rooms. Presumably other troopers had come around the side of the house.

"Did you make the call, sir?"

We parted. "Yes."

"Name?"

"Schuyler P. King."

The trooper wrote into his notebook. "Could you spell that first name, please?"

I did.

"Hmm. Not pronounced like it's spelled. What's that, German?"

"Dutch."

"Uh-huh. Did you know this man?"

"Yes. We were friends."

"Have any idea who could have done all this?"

"Whatever it was that killed him attacked me, too. It left when it heard you coming."

The trooper frowned. " 'It'?"

I considered how strange the entire truth would sound. "It was dark. Something . . . someone attacked me. It was dark, and I couldn't see much."

"You can't give a description?"

"It . . . he was big. Powerful."

"Weapon?" the trooper asked.

"None that I could see," I answered, while my mind's eye could envision nothing but those razorlike claws.

"Have any idea what could have done that to your friend's throat?"

"None. Do you?"

"Head's almost severed. The spinal cord looks broken, splintered. Whatever hit him, it was a hell of a blow."

"A bear?" I ventured.

The trooper shrugged. "Possible. There are grizzlies up in the National Forest area, and occasionally one wanders down here. But there aren't any claw marks on him. No bruises. It was quick. And bears don't do this much damage. They go right for the food. Anyway, we haven't had a bear incident in years. Are you saying that it was a bear that attacked you?"

"I don't know. All I know is that it was big and made strange noises."

The trooper nodded. He asked for my address and phone number and I gave it to him. Then he asked for particulars of what had led up to my making the emergency call, and I went over it for him, including all the details that came to mind. I stuck to the facts, but left out the emotional element. I told him about the breathing on the other end of the phone, but not about my reaction to it. I simply said it had sounded strange, almost feral.

"Like an animal or something," was the lame way I put it.

He kept nodding and writing. When I was through he nodded once more and said, "We'll be in contact, Mr. King. Thank you."

"Certainly."

Paramedics finally arrived, their only task to verify the fact of death so that the police could put in a call to the morgue. More troopers showed up, and plainclothesmen, too. A detective came up to me and introduced himself, and we went over the same ground again. More cars pulled up to the house, and soon the place was crawling. Strobe flashes came like quick, cold lightning.

Eventually a county vehicle pulled in and two morgue attendants gave the body a cursory once-over before they zippered it into a body bag, strapped it to a stretcher, and carried it out. I had a difficult time grappling with the notion that the lifeless object they were hauling away was once my friend Grant.

The homicide detectives scoured the place for clues while we stood and watched. They didn't find anything of interest. Somebody commented about the number of books. Grant had a great many books: standard reading list items, many works on history and politics, lots of paperback science fiction and fantasy, libraries of software manuals. Grant had always been interested in the occult, and that nebulous field was also well represented. Nobody seemed to take note of this. The detective team was too busy with fingerprint-dusting and other standard police procedures.

At last they were done, and we had to leave. Yellow plastic ribbon marked CRIME SCENE—KEEP OUT went across the doors and windows.

One detective who'd interviewed me smiled. "This must be pretty rough for you."

"Yes. Very. Don't you think there are some strange things about this case?"

He shrugged. "It looks like the work of a psychotic killer. Robbery might have been an afterthought. Did Mr. Barrington ever keep large sums of money around?"

"Not that I was aware of."

The detective (whose name I can't recall) looked back at the now-sealed house. "Nothing was taken— none of that expensive stereo or video equipment. No money, no jewelry. It is a little strange. That's why I say it was probably a psycho case."

I said, "Some wandering lunatic? Have there been cases like this recently?"

"Nope, none around here." He turned to face us. "Well, we'll be in touch, Mr. King. We might need some background on the victim." He smiled pleasantly at Sharon. "Good night." He walked off, but turned again with a lopsided grin.

"You're first name is Schuyler? Are you called Sky?"

"I spell it with an E."

"Sky King. That's a name out of my childhood."

"For a lot of people, apparently. It was a little before my time. I was named after my grandfather."

"Well, good night."

"Good night, Lieutenant."

Everyone left, and there was nothing to do but get in the car and go.

3

*T*HERE ARE TWO KINGS WHO ARE THE BANE OF MY life: Sky and Stephen. As to the first, the week does not go by in which someone Grant's age and/or a little younger doesn't throw "Sky King" in my face. I frankly can't remember the nineteen-fifties–vintage Saturday morning TV show by that name. I'm a tad too young, though I'm vaguely aware that the show featured a guy who flew the environs of his ranch in a twin-engine Beechcraft or some such contrivance. I'm used to brilliant wits (elide the *t* and *w*), who, with a smirk, pose the trivia question: "Where's Penny and Wheeler?" I've never bothered to ask, but my assumption is that they were supporting characters. I added the final superfluous vowel to my nickname mostly out of pique.

Regarding the second cross I bear, it must be admitted that King is a common name; but the famous-writer association is often made because I do look a little like Stephen King: dark hair and beard, glasses. Nope, no relation. Would that I were his only-begotten son. I'd kiss the man on the lips. Wouldn't you feel affectionately reverent toward someone who would eventually bequeath you untold wealth? (I'd also be reading up on untraceable poisons.)

*   *   *

There was no question of our trying to sleep. We went to my place and made coffee, then sat up most of the night and talked some. Mostly we stared at the walls. Sharon finally conked out on the couch, me in the easy chair. I woke up at quarter to nine and made a mad dash to Crowley Hall after splashing water on my face, gulping a glass of orange juice, and kissing Sharon good-bye.

The seminar was a minor disaster, but I was too numb to care. My students salvaged what they could from the ruins and patted my shoulder in commiseration as they left (I had told them there'd been a death in the family).

I went up to my office, looked through my department mail, found nothing of moment, and headed back to the house, thinking to get some sleep.

But when I got home there was a package sticking out of the storm door. It was from Grant.

The postmark was local, Saturday. I wondered why he hadn't just dropped it off. Maybe he was being watched?

I went in the house and got coffee started, then took a steak knife and cut the Mylar shipping tape that sealed the thick, padded mailing envelope. Inside was a white plastic box of the sort that floppy disks are packed in. Sure enough, floppies were inside, several of them, along with a typed note:

> Skye,
> If I don't talk to you before you get this, I'm sending these diskettes to you in case something happens to me. You read that right. I'm in trouble, and I really don't know if I can get out of it. I'm trapped, no escape.

They're out to get me. Who, you ask? Christ, if I could only offer some explanation that would not lead you to believe that I've turned stark raving Looney Tunes. But that's what the software is for. It might convince you.

Skye, use this software if and only if something happens to me. Run Ouija first. It's an interactive program that will explain the other software. It will also surprise the hell out of you. Repeat, if I'm still around, just put this stuff away and forget about it. However, if anything should befall me—like, the big D. I'm talking Death, here. If that happens, and, God, I hope it doesn't, boot up Ouija and follow its instructions. I have to leave town, but I'll be back Sunday night (the 11th) and will call you. I tried today but you weren't home. See you soon, I hope.

Grant

There were four disks of the newer 3.5" compact format. I normally used 5 ¼" floppies. There was, however, an accommodating drive in my computer for the smaller size, a bonus feature that had attracted me to the model. Puzzled and intrigued, I let Mr. Coffee drip away and went immediately to my study-alcove.

I took out Ouija and slipped it into the drive slot, fired up the computer, and installed the program on the hard disk. Then I typed "Ouija" and hit RETURN. What came on the screen was a very elaborate graphics display featuring strange typographical transmutations. Pretty. Grant was listed as the programmer. The usual copyright notices followed. Then a prompt asked me to enter my name. I did. The next instruction was, to say the least, enigmatic:

SHOW YOUR BADGE NUMBER:

What the hell? I hadn't a clue. I sat there with my head propped up over my fist, thinking furiously. What could Grant be driving at? Quite apart from the badge bit, why "show" and not "enter"?

I went back to the kitchen and poured myself coffee. As I was sluicing Half-and-Half into the cup, it hit me. I ran back to the computer and typed in:

WE DON'T GOT TO SHOW YOU NO STINKIN' BADGES!

Every so often we would rent *Treasure of the Sierra Madre* on video cassette and screen it together. Sometimes we'd invite friends and have a cinema party. That film, *Bringing Up Baby*, and a few other classics were perennial favorites. My inspiration paid off immediately. The screen read:

SKYE! YOU GOT THE PASS-PHRASE. GOOD THINK-ING, BUDDY. THERE WERE A COUPLE OF ALTERNA-TIVES IN CASE YOU DIDN'T TUMBLE TO THE FIRST QUESTION, BUT I KNEW YOU'D BE HIP TO B. TRA-VEN'S BADGES. HAD TO MAKE SURE IT WAS YOU. OKAY, SINCE YOU'RE RUNNING THIS SOFTWARE, THAT MUST MEAN I'M DEAD, GODDAMN IT. WHAT HAPPENED?

The cursor dropped to the next line and silently blinked at me, as though some response was expected. Again a strange feeling came over me: this had to be some diabolical practical joke on Grant's part. He had somehow faked his death, and now comes the payoff. I typed:

GRANT?

The cursor dropped again, and lines of character-strings spilled onto the screen, faster than anyone could type:

YEAH, IT'S ME. BUT IT'S NOT ME, THIS IS AN INTER-ACTIVE PROGRAM YOU'RE TALKING TO. IT'S ME IN THE SENSE THAT IT MIMICS MY PERSONALITY AND KNOWS MOST OF WHAT I KNOW. (IT DOESN'T KNOW, FOR INSTANCE, WHAT HAS HAPPENED TO ME SINCE I WROTE THIS PROGRAM.) IN THE FINAL ANALYSIS, IT IS ME, NOT JUST MY SURROGATE, SINCE THE "REAL" ME IS PRESUMABLY GONE. IN SHORT, YOU'RE TALKING TO GRANT, WHO IS NOW AN ARTI-FICIAL INTELLIGENCE PROGRAM. UNDERSTAND?

After a nonplussed moment or two, I responded:

UNDERSTOOD MORE LESS. BUT HOW ARE YOU DOING IT? HOW DID YOU WORK UP SUCH A SOPHIS-TICATED PROGRAM, AND HOW AM I RUNNING IT WITH THIS DESK TOP COMPUTER? GOD KNOWS I DON'T THINK IN BINARY, BUT I'M HIP ENOUGH TO KNOW THAT YOU CAN'T DO WHAT WE SEEM TO BE DOING WITH ONLY 2000K OF RAM AND A 100 MEGABYTE HARD DRIVE. OR AM I MISINFORMED?

The computer responded:

NO, YOU ARE NOT MISINFORMED. YOU'RE RIGHT, AI RESEARCH HASN'T GOT THIS FAR YET. BUT THIS PROGRAM IS NOT AN ORDINARY PIECE OF SOFTWARE. IT INCORPORATES RADICALLY NEW

ELEMENTS. OUIJA AND THE OTHER SOFTWARE IN THIS PACKET ARE THE PRODUCT OF BASIC RESEARCH IN AN ENTIRELY NEW FIELD OF KNOWLEDGE. IT'S SO NEW IT DOESN'T HAVE A NAME. SIMPLY PUT, IT'S A MARRIAGE OF MAGIC AND TECHNOLOGY.

All I could type was:

UH-HUH.

To which the computer replied:

METHINKS THOU'RT A BUT SKEPTICAL. UNDER-STANDABLE. GRANTED, IT SOUNDS WILD, WACKY—FLAKY, EVEN. BUT IT WORKS. JESUS H. CHRIST, DOES IT WORK.

OKAY. HOW?

DAMN GOOD QUESTION. VERY COMPLEX QUES-TION, BUT IT CAN BE OVERSIMPLIFIED THIS WAY: HOW ARE MAGIC SPELLS TRADITIONAL-LY CAST? ASIDE FROM THE USE OF MAGICAL OBJECTS OR TALISMANS, THE TWO MOST PRE-FERRED GIMMICKS ARE MAGIC WORDS—INCAN-TATIONS—AND INSCRIBED MAGICAL PATTERNS: PENTACLES, ARCANE DOODLES. RIGHT? OKAY. NOW, MAGIC IS A PRECISE ART, FOR ALL THE HOCUS-POCUS. FOR INSTANCE, YOU GOT-TA INSCRIBE A PENTAGRAM JUST RIGHT OR IT WON'T WORK. SAME GOES FOR INCANTATIONS. FLUB A LINE, AND THE SPELL FIZZLES. WELL, YOU CAN GET NO END OF PRECISION WITH GRAPHIC SOFTWARE, AND AT 20 MEGAHERTZ

YOU CAN REPEAT AN INCANTATION SEVERAL MILLION TIMES A SECOND. GOT IT SO FAR?

GOT IT [I typed]. BUT THERE'S AN UNSPOKEN AND VERY DUBIOUS ASSUMPTION HERE. WHAT YOU SAID SEEMS TO BE PREDICATED ON THE NOTION THAT MAGIC IS EFFICACIOUS, AN ASSUMPTION I'M JUST NOT WILLING TO GRANT . . . ER, GRANT.

AH, THE ETERNAL SKEPTICAL RATIONALIST. AND SKEPTICAL RATIONALISM'S NOT A BAD STANCE; QUITE UNDERSTANDABLE, IN FACT, WHAT WITH ALL THE NEW AGE MUSHHEADEDNESS GOING AROUND. BUT I'M TALKING ABOUT REAL MAGIC. NOW, HERE'S THE CRUX: MOST MAGIC IT MUST BE ADMITTED, IS NONSENSE. THERE IS SOME, HOWEVER, THAT IS MARGINALLY EFFECTIVE. THIS IS VERY HARD TO VERIFY OBJECTIVELY BECAUSE POSITIVE RESULTS TEND TO GET LOST IN STATISTICAL NOISE. BUT THE RESULTS ARE THERE. WHAT THIS NEW STUFF DOES IS TAKE THE MARGINAL EFFECTIVENESS AND APPLIES A LITTLE LEVERAGE. RATIONALIZES IT, MINIMIZES THE ERROR FACTOR. MORE THAN THAT. IT "HARDENS" MAGIC WITH A MATHEMATICAl RIGOR THAT MAGIC TRADITIONALLY LACKED. THERE WAS ALWAYS NUMEROLOGY, AND THAT WAS ON THE RIGHT TRACK, BUT IT WAS MOSTLY PYTHAGOREAN MYSTICAL JERKOFFERY. WITH ME?

MORE OR LESS [I typed back—at whom, I was in no way sure]. BUT I STILL CAN'T GET PAST THE STUMBLING BLOCK OF THE EFFICACY QUESTION. JUST WHAT MAGIC DOES WORK?

WELL [whoever it was responded], NOW WE'RE GETTING TO THE NITTY-GRITTY. RECENT ARCHAEOLOGICAL FINDS IN THE MIDDLE EAST HAVE UNEARTHED A LOT OF NEW STUFF—CODICES OF ANCIENT GRIMORIES, BOOKS DEALING WITH ANCIENT MAGIC THAT HAVE BEEN KNOWN FOR CENTURIES BUT ONLY IN FRAGMENTARY OR DISTORTED FORM. THE SPELLS YOU GET OUT OF BOOKS ON WITCHCRAFT IN ANY PUBLIC LIBRARY—SOME OF THAT'S THE GENUINE ARTICLE ALL RIGHT, BUT MOST OF IT WAS DELIBERATELY DISTORTED IN ANTIQUITY, BY HIGH PRIESTS AND COURT MAGICIANS AND THE LIKE, FOR REASONS OF SECURITY. CLASSIFIED MATERIAL. THE REAL MCCOY WAS EVENTUALLY LOST, AND MAGIC DIED OUT. EVER WONDER WHY THE OLD TESTAMENT, FOR INSTANCE, TAKES EFFICACIOUS MAGIC AS A GIVEN? PHARAOH'S MAGICIANS WORKED THE RIGHT STUFF; IT'S JUST THAT MOSES (OR AARON, I GUESS) WAS THE BETTER MAGICIAN. OKAY, BELOVED INFIDEL, MAYBE EXODUS IS MORE FICTION THAN FACT, BUT IT JUST MAY BE THAT THE "NONFICTION NOVEL" IS OLDER THAN TRUMAN CAPOTE. IN ANY EVENT, THE OLD STUFF WORKS, IF YOU DO IT RIGHT. FOR INSTANCE, THIS PROGRAM IS BASED IN PART ON A NECROMANTIC EVOCATION OF THE DEAD THAT DATES TO THE TIME OF THE FOUNDATION OF THE PERSIAN EMPIRE. EH? AM I STARTING TO BREACH ANY OF THOSE FORMIDABLE RATIONALIST BULWARKS OF YOURS YET?

I typed "No" but did not press ENTER. I hit the backspace key and cleared the screen, then, after a moment's reflection, banged out:

O GREAT MAGUS, PRAY TELL—WHAT THE FUCK HAS ALL THIS TO DO WITH ANYTHING?

I'M GETTING TO THAT. YOU'RE FROM MISSOURI RIGHT? THE "SHOW ME" STATE. (An obscene response to that always occurred to me, but I let it pass.) I'M GOING TO HAVE TO DEMONSTRATE, BUT IN ORDER TO REALLY UNDERSTAND WHAT'S GOING ON, YOU'RE GOING TO HAVE TO PLUG INTO THE NET.

"AND WHAT NET IS THAT?" OUR HERO ASKED OF THE COOLLY SMILING FU MANCHU.

<GRIN> OH, GOOD ONE. THE NET IS MAGICNET. IT'S ALSO CALLED THE MANDALA, THE TANGLED-WEB AND A BUNCH OF OTHER THINGS. IT'S NOT COMPUSERVE. IT'S NOT LIKE ANY OTHER COMPUTER NETWORK YOU'VE EXPERIENCED. I WANT YOU TO PLUG INTO IT. THERE'S SOMETHING I WANT YOU TO DO FOR ME, IF YOU'RE WILLING.

WHAT'S THAT?

IT, TOO, WILL TAKE SOME EXPLAINING. I'M GOING TO CHARGE YOU WITH A QUEST, MY SON. YOU WILL SEEK THE HOLY GRAIL.

ARE YOU GOING TO ASK ME MY FAVORITE COLOR?

BLUE. NO, YELLOW! ARRRRGGGGGHHHH! RIGHT, BUT THIS IS SERIOUS SKYE.

[I keyed] IF YOU SAY SO.

I SAY SO. IT IS IMPERATIVE THAT YOUR MISSION BE COMPLETED SUCCESSFULLY, OR THE UNIVERSE AS WE KNOW IT MIGHT VERY WELL CEASE TO EXIST. AT THE VERY LEAST, IT WILL CHANGE FOR THE WORSE.

At that point I burst out laughing. The impetus, I suspect, was part hysteria, part relief. I got up and walked in circles, trying to overcome a dizzy feeling of unreality. Then, very suddenly, the image of Grant's gaping throat presented itself, a horrid tableau in my mind's terrified eye. Instantly, I sobered up and sat down. The universe as I had known it was already one with Nineveh and Tyre. Something bizarre had entered my world, that was absolute fact. At this point I did not know much. However, if red-eyed monsters could exist, as indeed they seemed to, I couldn't rule anything out, however far fetched it sounded or however dubious its source, this oddly behaving computer being no exception.

The screen read:

WHAT'S SO GODDAMN FUNNY?

SORRY [I typed—then something hit me]. WAIT A MINUTE. HOW DID YOU KNOW I WAS LAUGHING?

UH ... I DON'T REALLY KNOW HOW I KNOW, BUT I DO. I CAN'T SEE OR HEAR YOU, BUT I CAN SENSE YOU SOMEHOW. REMEMBER, I'M A SPIRIT THAT YOU'VE EVOKED. THE PROGRAM'S NOT CALLED OUIJA FOR NOTHING. ANYWAY, TO DO WHAT WE HAVE TO DO, WE NEED SOME BETTER HARDWARE. CAN YOU GET YOUR HANDS ON A LAPTOP COMPUTER?

SHARON HAS A LAPTOP [I answered]. I DON'T KNOW WHETHER IT HAS A HARD DISK. SHE MIGHT BE WILLING TO LEND IT—THEN AGAIN, SHE USES IT A LOT.

CAN YOU SPRING FOR ONE?

CHRIST. I SUPPOSE SO, IF IT'S REALLY NECESSARY. ACTUALLY, I HAVE BEEN TOYING WITH THE NOTION OF GETTING ONE.

THEN GET ONE, AND A GOOD ONE, TOP OF THE LINE, WITH THE LATEST MICROCHIP. I DON'T CARE ABOUT THE MAKE, JUST AS LONG AS IT RUNS DOS, THE PREFERRED OPERATING SYSTEM OF DISCRIMINATING MAGICIANS. THE HARDWARE CAN BE JAPANESE, AMERICAN, KOREAN, GENERIC PACIFIC RIM—IT DOESN'T MATTER.

I sighed. "Shit," I said to myself. "This is the most insane, wacked-out—" I shrugged, then keyed in:

OKAY. WHAT ELSE DO YOU WANT ME TO DO?

The cursor danced across the screen.

THAT'S THE SPIRIT, GOOD BUDDY. NOW, HERE'S MY PLAN . . . (FADE TO BLACK). . . .

4

THE PRICE TAG, INCLUDING TAX, FOR ALL THE items on Grant's shopping list climbed into the middle four-figures. I invoked generic supernatural forces (whose existence I was now beginning to take for granted), giving thanks for plastic cash and an enabling hike in my available credit line via a quick 800-number phone call. Fortunately the plastic money demigods considered me good for it.

Included in the fancy new hardware was a voice synthesizer of the type available to blind computer users. I was skeptical, but Grant said to go ahead and hook it up.

"Hear me now?" the synthetic voice from the speaker asked. I typed:

YOU SOUND LIKE SOMETHING OUT OF A BAD SCI-FI FLICK BUT I CAN DEFINITELY UNDERSTAND YOU.

"We'll have to work on that. By the way, I can hear you fine. Just talk normally."

"Huh? Why couldn't you hear me before?"

"Don't know."

I glanced at my watch. "It's only been two hours since

I left for the computer place. Any idea as to what has changed?"

The voice was silent for a moment, then opined: "You're right, things are changing. I feel more in touch with the physical universe. Rather, with the universe you inhabit, which is physical."

"You're in a different universe?"

"Well, sort of."

"Sort of? What's it like?"

"Hard to say."

"Big help."

"Sorry, Skye. Wish I could do better. There are simply no words for what I want to describe."

"Okay, don't try. But tell me this, spirit. If you can hear me, why can't I hear you without all this gadgetry? Why can't you simply . . . haunt me?"

"This is an official haunt," the voice said. "Seriously, it's not easy crossing the barrier between the living and the dead. That's why you don't see ghosts walking up and down the street. I guess the answer is that it's easier for sense impressions to permeate from your side to my side rather than the other way. That make sense?"

"More or less," I said. "It sounds okay on the face of it, but I'll bet you dollars to ectoplasm it won't bear scrutiny."

"I don't know all the ins and outs yet," Grant said. (It was at this point that I began to accept the voice as belonging to at least a simulacrum of Grant himself.) "I'm still pretty new at this being-dead business. Okay, let's get back to the issue of my recent demise. What exactly happened?"

"Wondering when you were going to ask. Okay, I'll give you all the gruesome details. But there's another thing that bothers me. If you're Grant's ghost, why don't you know what happened?"

"Another good question," Grant's spirit said. "And notwithstanding what I said earlier, I think I do know what happened—vaguely. It's sort of like a lingering, half-forgotten memory."

"But if you're artificial, not a real ghost—"

"I am a real ghost, but I'm not quite your traditional ghost. I'm partly an artifact, infused with elements of the real Grant's . . . well, 'soul' would be the word."

" 'The real Grant.' Now that you brought it up, aside from being dead, where exactly is the real Grant?"

"I'm not going to even speculate where that sucker is. If he's anywhere. That's all you're going to get from me on that issue. For now, at least."

"It will have to suffice," I said. "Now the gruesome details."

I told him.

The voice was silent for a while. Then: "Yeah, it was as I feared. Merlin made good on his threat to anyone who was going to rock the boat."

"Who is Merlin?"

"We'll get to him later."

"Okay," I said. "What was it that got you?"

"A supernatural version of a professional hit man. There was a contract out on me."

"Yeah, but what was it?"

"Basically a demon."

"I was thinking more along the lines of were-wolf."

"Simply another form of a demon. Werewolves, ghosts, unicorns, dragons. Every critter you can imagine and some you can't is on the Net."

"Grant, tell me what the Net is. Explain it."

"I'll try, but what you have to get straight is that no one completely understands it yet. First, let's get moving. I'll talk on the way."

I stood up. "We're going somewhere?"

"Why do you think I wanted the laptop? Pack me up and let's go."

The computer and synthesizer together were too big for a standard computer case, so I had bought a black nylon carrying bag with a shoulder strap. It accommodated both devices easily, along with connecting cable, the computer's operating manual, and a few odds and ends. The original diskettes, their data now recorded on the laptop's hard disk, I had erased at Grant's behest. Then, still obeying instructions but under protest, I made copies of all my data files and reformatted the hard disk of my desktop computer, effectively wiping it clean. When I asked Grant if he wasn't afraid of the laptop's disk crashing with no backup copies of the software extant, he said the stuff was too sensitive to leave lying around. Anyway, the laptop would be "magically protected," he said.

"And ditto your desktop," Grant added.

"But it's clean."

"No, just reformatted. Any hacker could reconstruct the data, but protection spells will make that a little problematical."

"Yeah," I said dully, wondering how anything could sound more absurd. *Protection spells*, indeed.

I took a shower and put on fresh clothes—a heavy red plaid shirt, jeans, hiking boots—and pulled on my leather flying jacket. Duffel bag slung over my shoulder, I left the house with the laptop operating on its batteries and a program named MagicNet running. Did this mean that Ouija would be inactive? No, came the reply. "Multitasking."

Multitasking. Thank you, Mnemosyne, cybernetic Muse, for that and numerous other gifts to the language.

The weather had turned a little chillier, but the late-afternoon sun was out, and the air, laden with rich smells of a renewing earth, still said spring.

According to instructions, I started walking north along College Avenue.

"No one knows who developed the original software for the Net," the voice from the bag said. "The whole thing is shrouded in myth. There're various stories. Some say the software came out of MIT, some say a research lab in Israel. It's also been attributed to a legendary microchip-reprogramming artist—a 'chipper'—known only as the Nutcracker. All of that along with the usual Department-of-Defense-origin rumor."

"Isn't there always? Or the CIA."

"The government hasn't wormed itself into this yet, as far as we know."

"Or any other governments?"

"No. For years there were stories about the Soviets doing research in the occult and ESP, but that's got to be hogwash. Can you imagine dialectical materialists spending their hard-earned rubles on Ouija boards and tarot cards?"

"Why not?" I said. "If they thought there may have been a possible defense coup in it. It wouldn't have been the first time ideology was bypassed for reasons of expediency."

"I doubt it. They may have dabbled, but it couldn't have amounted to much, or we'd be speaking Russian. No, the bureaucratic-autocratic mind can't grasp this sort of thing. Even I have trouble sometimes. I have to admit, the idea of the Net strains credulity. It's always in the back of my mind that the whole thing is a shared hallucination."

"Which you've snared me into," I said. "Thanks a whole lot, Grant."

"You're very welcome. Then again, laptop computers usually don't speak with the voices of one's murdered friends, do they?"

Now that he mentioned it, I had been noticing that the ersatz space-alien voice from the synthesizer box had modulated a bit. It sounded a little more human, and, unless I was imagining things, was beginning to take on some of the intonations and inflections of Grant's voice.

"Are we at Mulberry Street yet?"

"Just ahead," I said.

"Turn left on Mulberry."

"You're the autocrat," I said. "Grant, you've been dancing around the main issue. Just what the hell *is* the Net? Give."

Grant answered, "The Net is just what it sounds like. It's a computer network, a linkup between computers, magical computers. But it's more than a communications network. It's . . . well, it's an alternative reality."

"Interesting. Some other dimension?"

"The concept's hard to label. 'Dimension' might be as good a handle as any, cliché though it is. The notion of parallel universes is useful to bear in mind, but that's not really what it's all about either. What's being created on the Net is an alternative reality, a skein of experience and perception that, at present, interweaves with conventional experience and perception. The key point's this: the Net is being created and sustained by the magic contained in these spells. If it's a parallel universe, it's one that was empty before all this started. As I said, the alternate-world scenario is only useful to a point. There are any number of philosophical ramifications to all this, which I won't go into now."

I passed a pretty white birch, the sight of it reassuring me that the natural universe was real, surely more real than the malarkey Grant was spewing. But doubt already gnawed at my coziest assumptions.

"And this whole thing," I said, "this brave new cosmos, created and controlled by—for want of a better term—computer hackers."

"Right, but a special kind of hacker. Your average programmer can't develop this software, nor can your cleverest chipper or backdoor cracker. Remember, not just mere computer technology is involved. It takes a special talent, not only to create the software, but to use it effectively."

"I seem to be using it without too much trouble," I pointed out.

"There was some question beforehand as to whether you could or not. But as it turns out, you have a modicum of talent."

"Are we talking paranormal talent? I'm some incipient psychic?"

"Paranormal, maybe. 'Psychic' is a meaningless husk of a word, if it ever meant anything. Tabloid word. I'm talking about a talent for intuitive metaphysics. A sharp eye that can penetrate the veil of Maya and see through to the core of things."

"Which is?"

"That remains to be seen. How far along are we on Mulberry?"

I looked. "The five-hundred block."

"You should be near it."

"Near what?"

As soon as I said it I saw the house. It was a many-gabled Gothic beauty, complete with turret, widow's walk, cupola, and leaded windows, painted white with light blue trim. The corner property on which it sat was surrounded by a high spiked wrought iron fence. I had walked this street for years and had never seen the place before.

"That's Sima Berkowitz's place. Go ahead, she's probably expecting you. If I know Sima, she already knows pretty much what happened."

It occurred to me that I hadn't checked the papers for the news story of Grant's murder. The local paper was published in the evening, but the nearest big-city morning editions might have carried it. Might not have, though. The lead time had been short, and College Green was an isolated little island in the middle of a vast agrarian sea. News traveled slowly.

There was an iron gate, executed in fancy scroll-work, blocking steps that mounted to the front walk. A sign over a pearl button instructed RING BELL. I rang.

In a moment the lock on the gate buzzed. I pushed and the gate opened. I closed it behind me.

For all that its architecture was associated with haunt-ed houses, the place looked bright and cheery, freshly painted and optimistic. It did not brood. Its eaves harbored no dark secrets. But there was something else strange else about it. There was an anomalous quality here. It looked like no other house in town. It was showy, quirky, too much like something you might encounter in a Hollywood back lot. And I was damned if the gaudy thing had been there two minutes ago.

But Skye King knew no fear. He had the miracle of modern electronics at his beck and call.

5

THE DOOR HAD A PONDEROUS WROUGHT IRON knocker. I hefted it, then let it settle back gently against the white-painted wood. No need to knock. Somebody knew I was here.

At length the door was opened by a heavyset, dark-haired woman with dark brown eyes. Her hair was short, done in odd tufts and swirls. She had on a loose black dress and black shoes. The only spot of color on her was a gold necklace with one of the signs of the zodiac hanging from it. I thought it might be Leo, but wasn't sure.

She looked the slightest bit apprehensive.

"Yes?" she said.

"I'm Schuyler King. A friend of Grant Barrington?"

She nodded gravely. "Something's happened to Grant, hasn't it?"

Her look said that she was hoping against hope something hadn't.

"I'm afraid so," I said. "He's dead."

She let out a long breath, then frowned, as though berating herself for not knowing better. Then, almost inaudibly: "Oh, my."

"Gone but not forgotten, Sima."

She gave a little jump, then looked curiously at the carrying bag.

The synthesized voice went on, "Or, should I say, forgotten but not gone?"

Sima stared at the bag for a moment, then looked up at me. "A necromantic spell?"

The voice said, "Good guess, Sima."

Sima leaned forward a bit, still holding on to the door. "Grant, is that really you? It doesn't sound like you . . . well, maybe sort of, in a way."

"It's me. And I'm deader than a sail cat on Route 22."

"You told me you were working on a ghost spell, but I never really thought you'd actually do it."

"I never thought I'd be using it on myself. It seems to work, though."

"I'll say. Grant, what *happened* to you? Last night the Net was throwing off all sorts of weird vibes. Nobody knew what was going on."

"Merlin got to me. One of his goblins did, rather."

"That bastard."

"You're telling me."

Sima Berkowitz sighed. Then she gestured to me. "Please come in."

I went in.

The place seemed smaller inside, and the more I looked about, the more I was convinced that that the interior was smaller than the exterior, paradoxical though it sounds. Why or how this could be so, I did not venture to guess.

Sima Berkowitz was a collector of curios. Statuettes were numerous, favoring Egyptian images. Cats, lots of cats, the thin, mystic-eyed breed that moused the banks of the Nile. Feline subjects were overrepresented in paintings and prints on the walls. There were other statuettes, some of Egyptian gods, others less identifiable. Candles abounded, tall ones, stubby ones, votives, decoratives. Many were lighted. The place glowed with candlelight. Scents were many: I smelled bayberry, spice, and sandalwood.

Something rubbed against my leg and I looked down. Graymalkin, friendly to strangers. On the back of the sofa, eyeing me dispassionately, sat an aloof, soot black Pyewacket. Sima introduced me to her cats as I stood in the living room, taking the place in.

One wall was devoted to prints with fantasy themes: unicorns, dragons, haunted castles. The house contained a great variety of bric-a-brac. However, looking at it another way, lots of it was of a piece; there was a theme here. The theme was the supernatural, the unseen world, the astral plane.

"Grant's mentioned you once or twice," Sima told me.

"In terms of highest praise," Grant put in.

"I'm sure. What do you do, Sima?"

"Work for the university."

"What else?" Grant said.

"What else," Sima sighed. "Around here, anyway. Can I get you tea, Skye?"

"Nothing for me, thanks. You have a nice place here."

"Thank you. I'm a pack rat. Look at this clutter."

"Lots of interesting pieces. Those crystals . . ."

"From a dry cave in Nevada. Mined them myself, had a jeweler polish and mount them."

"Imagine. Are they supposed to have any power?"

Sima smiled. "I think you're patronizing me. They're pure quartz, and they have the all powers accruing to pure quartz. Those others are calcite, and they have calcite powers."

I smiled back. "Well, crystal power is a New Age crotchet, and I assumed. Sorry."

"Never assume. But I will tell you that everything of the earth has power. Everything, as does the earth itself."

Sima sat on the easy chair that made an L with the sofa. She gestured me to the sofa. I walked over.

Yellow-eyed Pyewacket, still perched in the middle of the sofa's back, noted my approach. I chose the extreme end, near Sima's chair. The cat did not move but continued to watch me. I set the carrying bag beside me, unzipped it, and retrieved the notebook-size computer, which I laid on the parquet coffee table.

"How's it going, Sima?" Grant asked.

"This is so strange," Sima said, shaking her head. "Grant, I should be asking you questions."

"I know, but don't. Skye tried, but didn't get very far. I'm not even sure I exist, in the normal sense."

"You sound real enough."

"Maybe. But there are other things to talk about. Like Merlin."

"Who is Merlin?" I asked.

"He's . . . oh, I guess you'd call him the sysop of MagicNet," Sima said.

"The what?"

"Short for 'system operator,' " Grant told me. "Sima, Skye doesn't do any networking."

"Not even on the commercial networks?"

"No, never did," I said. "It costs, and I don't have the time anyway."

"You're wise," Sima said. "Networking can be addictive."

"Many's the person who's drowned in a networking time sink," Grant said. "Anyway, that's what Merlin is, but nobody elected him. He sort of took over."

"What's this guy's real name?"

"Merlin is his real name. Merlin Jones. Lloyd Merlin Jones, to be exact. He prefers to be called Merlin."

"What is he?"

"Eh?"

"What does he do besides lord it over MagicNet?"

"Oh. Well, nobody knows much about him. He's a hacker, to be sure. And his input into the software that controls the Net has been considerable."

"I thought nobody knows who developed the software."

"That's right, but it's been tinkered with endlessly, as all software is. Merlin's done a lot of it. Improved it greatly, too. That I'll give him."

Sima said, "But now he thinks he owns it. In fact, he now claims to have discovered the magic it's based on and to have developed the original software."

Grant added, "And he considers himself liege lord of the kingdom of MagicNet, expecting us all to kowtow."

I said, "Grant, something tells me that you and this Jones character didn't quite see eye to eye."

"Something tells you quite rightly. Jones is all egalitarianism on the surface, all smarmy psychobabble and trendy cant, but scratch him with a feather and you reveal him for the tin Hitler he really is. He's horrendously bright, there's no doubt, but he's convinced that gives him some right to call the shots for us lesser mortals."

"And you had a run-in with him. Over what?"

"Oh, lots of things." Grant's voice made a sound not unlike a slow exhale. (But . . . breath?) "This is going to be hard to explain. A lot of the bones of contention have to do with how the Net is run, and that involves software. And then there's policy concerning who gets admitted into the network, how much should be kept from the public, how much should be let out. That sort of thing. Political issues."

"But you did have a run-in," I said. "And as a result, he sicced his goblin on you. My question is, was it a real preexisting goblin or was it something created by computers?"

"That's part of what's at issue. We really don't know what those things are, the things you summon to do your bidding. They may be software wildlife."

"Software wildlife?"

"Yeah, strange concept. Goes something like this. The data network—cyberspace, some people call it—can be considered an artificial natural environment—if you'll pardon the oxymoron."

"That's not an oxymoron," I said. "That's a flat contradiction in terms."

"So sue me. Anyway, you've heard of computer viruses, which are a form of life, artificially created. Now, think of computer programs breaking off little pieces of themselves, fissioning into discrete, independent units that have viability on their own. Software bacteria, organisms. Imagine these organisms evolving over time into more complex organisms, then species differentiating, each finding its ecological niche."

"Over time? Has there been enough time for evolution to take place?"

"Not in realtime. But in terms of cyberspace-time, plenty. Millions of years, equivalent."

"I see. Does Merlin think these forces you've made contact with are software wildlife?"

"He's vague on the issue."

"What do you think he thinks they are?"

"Manifestations of the self. You see, it all hinges on what you believe about magic. Merlin takes the New Age view. Well, maybe that's not the right term. Anyway, he sees magic as a function of psi. Extrasensory power. ESP. In other words, it's all in the mind. There is the opposing view, that magic is what it is, a way of manipulating an unseen but objective reality, a reality that might be inhabited by independent entities."

"Like ghosts and goblins."

"Like ghosts and goblins," Sima said. "And demons."

"Demons," I said, nodding.

"Yup. Simply put, that could be what they are," Grant said. "Ancient powers, ancient evils."

"Do you believe that's what killed you?"

Grant thought about it. "I really don't know. Something evil did the deed, though. What's the difference whether it's of recent origin or ancient?"

"But you believe it was something supernatural . . . or at least fantastical in nature. Right?"

"Right. Unless it was a psychopathic Amway salesman."

I grunted a perfunctory laugh.

"I know it's a hard concept to get around," Sima said, "especially for someone—" She broke off and looked toward the front door.

"Something?" I asked.

"Probably the paperboy."

She got up and went toward the entry hall.

"Are you following all this?" Grant wanted to know.

47

"So far," I said. "I'm a little sketchy on details. What else is on the Net besides demons?"

"Oh, demons are only a small part of what there is. With the right magic you can create anything. You can create your own demons, if you want to. They probably wouldn't be able to hurt anyone, though. That takes black magic, and that involves pacts with the powers of evil. Otherwise, you can create anything, from unicorns to . . . well, take Sima's house, for instance. What you saw outside was not real. I take it you copped to that."

"Yeah, fairly early on. But not the inside, though?"

"I like the inside of my house the way it is," Sima said, returning after having opened the front door and closing it again. She was carrying a rolled-up newspaper. "Besides, doing inside-outside magical domiciles is tricky. I'm no hacker, just a computer user. Afternoon paper came."

She sat down, unrolled the paper, and began scanning it.

"Anything about me?" Grant asked.

"That's what I'm looking for. Here it is. 'A Westonville man was found dead in his home last night, the victim of a possible marauding bear attack, a state police spokesman reported early this morning. Police investigators are not ruling out foul play, however . . . ' "

"Bear attack," I said without much inflection.

"Mundane reality strikes again," Grant said.

I looked at the computer. "Grant, what do you mean?"

"Well, I'm not sure what I mean. The Net has rarely impinged on workaday reality. But when it does, there seems to be a self-correcting process that comes into play."

"I'm still a bit unclear."

"Maybe it's a conspiracy. Maybe somebody's . . ." The voice trailed off. "Don't want to get unnecessarily paranoid. Skye, I don't know what it is. It may be that the police are simply not capable of admitting the possibility of paranormal events. Psychotic killer or marauding bear, those are the only two rational explanations for what went on, by their lights. What else are they going to tell the press? 'By the way, it might have been a demon'?"

I shrugged. "No, I guess not."

"Did you let on anything?"

"Nothing at all," I said.

"Well, okay. All they know is that something hit that place like a tornado."

"Or a bear."

"Uh-huh. Skye, do you think it was a bear?"

"Listen to this," Sima said. " 'This incident coincides with a report earlier this year of one Crawford county man who was allegedly mauled by a black bear—' " Sima laughed. " 'Allegedly,' I love that."

"Animal rights," Grant said. "Presumption of innocence."

Sima giggled, then resumed reading. " . . . 'allegedly mauled by a black bear while hunting in the Allegheny National Forest region.' "

"Wonder who was hunting," Grant said.

"Doesn't say. Yeah. Uh, it doesn't elaborate. The story isn't very long."

"I'm not worth the column space," Grant said with a heavy sigh.

"Grant, could it have been an animal?" Sima asked.

"Ask Skye. He saw the thing."

"I saw a pair of red eyes. Whatever it was, it was big. And mean."

"God. Were you scared?"

It was my turn to laugh. "The nightmares I had after were worse. When it was happening I was numb. It was . . ."

I let silence slide by.

"Must be hard to talk about," Grant said.

"It was unreal," I said. Then I must have scowled. "You were the one killed, for Christ's sake. What was it like to . . .? Oh, hell. I don't even know how to ask the question."

"It's a little vague in my mind, though I think 'stark terror' covers it nicely," Grant said.

"Yeah." I looked at Sima. "Stark terror."

"I'm scared," Sima said. "I don't mind admitting it."

"Are you in any danger?" I asked her.

"I don't know. I don't think so. I doubt that Merlin has anything against me."

"I don't think Sima is in any danger for the moment," Grant said. "Though she is my friend and has backed me in the past against Jones."

"I'd do it again," Sima said. "Thing is, I'm no match for Merlin. He's good. He's very good. And he's dangerous."

"Is there anyone who can stand up to him?" I asked. "Does he have a match?"

"Grant," Sima said.

"I thought," Grant said. "I was wrong. He got through my defenses easily enough. I think I know how he did it, and it was pretty slick. No, all things being equal, Jones is going to be hard to beat."

"We're going to try to beat him?" I said.

"That's up to you, Skye. I'll need your help to do it."

Pyewacket had stirred, tightroping across the back of the sofa to within sniffing distance of me. I turned my head. The cat brought its charcoal nose up close to my sleeve without quite touching.

"He likes you," Sima said. "Unusual."

"Yes, it's unusual for anyone to like Skye."

"You hush."

"Please, you're talking to a dead person. Sorry, one of the Physiologically Challenged."

"Oh, groan."

Pyewacket, having taken my measure and found me wanting, was done with me. He jumped off the sofa back and ran into the dining room.

"What's up to me?" I said.

"Well, this," Grant went on. "You have on the hard disk of this computer a certain program. It's called Ragnarok, and if it's run within proximity of Merlin's main computer, the one he keeps MagicNet constantly running on, it might do the trick."

"What trick?"

"It'll change the universe."

Graymalkin was at my left shin, rubbing back and forth, leaving his trace, his scent, a pheromone bar code that cataloged me as part of his personal chattel, here in his territorial domain.

I let out a long exhale.

"I think I'm going to go home," I said.

"Might not be such a good idea. You should rest, though. Think about things first. There's no hurry. The situation has stabilized for the moment."

I felt tired. Lack of sleep was finally getting to me. "I have to go home."

"But you have no protections there," Grant said.

"Grant's right," Sima said. "Stay here. I'll put you up for a few days."

"Nice of you to offer," I said. "But I really should be leaving."

Sima shrugged. "Whatever. You're welcome, though."

"As I said, kind of you. No, I have a number of things I have to do now."

"Skye? Take Sima up on her invitation. Take it easy for tonight."

"No, thanks," I said decisively.

"Skye, you really hadn't better do that. You have software protection, and Sima's spells are working, too."

I reached toward the computer.

"Skye, don't—"

I switched the thing off. The screen went dark, and I pushed it down, locking it into place and closing up the machine.

I let out a long breath. Then I looked at Sima. She regarded me with a kind of detached curiosity, as if only mildly interested in what I would do next.

"I've had enough," I said.

She nodded. "I can see."

"This has gone far enough. I have to get back to reality."

She nodded again. "If you have to, sure."

"I'm going to go now."

"It was nice meeting you."

I packed up everything, stood, and slung the bag over my shoulder. "My pleasure."

Sima showed me out without our exchanging another word. I stopped on the front porch to look back. She smiled faintly as she closed the door.

The door shut, and I headed for the street.

I was about ten paces away from the steps when I realized the house had changed. I stopped and looked back. It was smaller and needed a paint job. Gone were the Victorian touches, the cupolas, the turrets, the widow's walk. Now the place was just a dirty white frame two-story with clapboard siding.

6

*I*T WAS GOOD TO BE OUTDOORS AGAIN. THE PHYSI-cal world, the mundane world of my experience, seemed sharp-edged and poignantly real. Familiar sights reassured me, the pavement felt good and hard under my feet. Bare branches made pretty scrollwork against the sky and to my nose came smells of spring and of the earth and greening things, and the smells were much stronger than before.

I didn't want to think about anything that had happened in the last twenty-four hours, didn't want to deal with any of the various ramifications, significances, signs, portents, or meanings pertaining thereto. Nor with any analytical interpretations of any of the above. I wanted pure, unambiguous sense-data. Patches of blue, swatches of brown and green, the patterns of lichen on a rock, the network of cracks against the sidewalk. Sense-data, and only sense-data. Only these were real.

I retraced my steps, still carrying the damned bag and its contents, resolved never to turn on the laptop computer again, or at least to delay such an action. I'd put it in the closet, forget about it for a couple of months. After a suitable period of neglect, I would take it out again and reformat its hard disk. Yes, that's what I'd do. And I'd have myself a nifty little computer, handy for use on working vacations—in case I ever took a working vacation—or for doing research at the library. Handy. Nifty.

A cloud covered the sun and something happened to my mood. Footsteps came from behind.

I stopped, turned. The sidewalk was empty behind me. I then heard a strange birdcall. It was a kind of chittering laugh, unfamiliar, mischievous, possibly malevolent.

I shook my head. No, nothing.

I resumed walking, trying not to think, trying to prevent the wheels from turning. Possibly Sharon would like to go out to dinner again tonight. I certainly didn't feel like cooking. Didn't know if there was anything in the house to cook. Could always go shopping, though. I'd been wanting to try making *puttanesca* sauce—tomatoes, anchovies, olives, capers. Whore's sauce. It would be good over linguine with a lively Bardolino, or possibly a Valpolicella. No, too light for such a strong sauce. A well-chilled Barolo, from the Piedmont, would be the perfect complement.

Oh, shit.

I felt strange. My heart was racing and I felt clammy all over. Sounds seemed amplified. Everything around me murmured and hummed. A soft spring breeze rioted in the trees, making a horrid din. The distant toot of a horn became a honk of some great bird of prey; the sudden roar of a downshifting trailer truck came like the primordial bellow of a dinosaur. Grass fought noisily with weeds in the greening strip of earth running between sidewalk and street.

I was afraid. Of what, I didn't know, but a cold fear overcome me. I tried to walk faster but something held me back. My feet splatted through an unseen mire, a hideous sinkhole that sucked me down. The sky darkened and I wondered if I was going to pass out. It occurred to me that I might be having a heart attack.

I became convinced that a heart attack was either imminent or had already arrived, already had me calipered in its vise. My chest constricted, its muscles tightening into a hard cuirass, a breastplate of pain. My breath came in gasps.

I dropped the bag, stopped, bent over, hands braced against my knees, head down as far as I could get it, trying to force blood into it. I remained in that position until I was sure I would not pass out.

I finally straightened up. I belched, loudly. Again. Several more times.

Gastric distress? Maybe. I felt a little better for acknowledging the possibility. Maybe the nausea was due to an upset stomach. The nervousness, the uncertainty. The weirdness; they'd all taken their toll.

I picked up the bag and walked on. The fear, however, remained. I was convinced someone was following me, just out of sight, around the last corner I had turned, stepping purposefully, inexorably, shadowing me, dogging my every pace.

A fast car roared by and startled me. I stopped and looked behind once again, still convinced that I was the object of a studied and calculating pursuit. I turned, and began to jog, and kept jogging until I got home.

Inside the house, safe. Safe—I thought. I hoped.

But four walls around me didn't help. Noises from upstairs, creaks—footsteps? I got out a kitchen knife and climbed the stairs.

No one around; all three bedrooms were unoccupied except for lingering traces of the person who lived here, eidolons of myself, along with a few stray electromagnetic waves still propagating from Sharon's latest overnight stay. I came back downstairs, worried now about the basement.

If there was a flashlight in the kitchen drawers, it successfully eluded my search. I gave up and opened the cellar door, flicked on the light, and stared down. The bare concrete floor at the bottom had nothing to say to me. Not even the furnace had a comment, and it was usually as voluble as hell.

I turned off the light and shut the door. Something was wrong with me. I did not usually act this way, have these unfocused anxieties, these sudden panics. Nor had I ever experienced paranoia, true paranoia— the feeling that somebody or something was watching, waiting, plotting.

That feeling did not go away. It resisted my taking no less than three 500mg tablets of acetaminophen. It laughed off a hot shower. (Strangely enough, the shower curtain did not taunt me with a shadow-puppet Tony Perkins in wig and housecoat, butcher knife raised high. Not that I cared one way or the other. I would have welcomed a cross-dressing but all-too-human serial killer into my bath. Confused humans I could deal with. The thing that was out to get me was inhuman, vast and shadowy.)

The haunting persisted through two bottles of Beck's dark and one of Corona. I had no hard drugs in the house, no "downers," no tranquilizers. I needed the industrial-strength variety. There was only one way to get it.

I phoned a woman I knew, a clinical psychologist. We had dated once, nothing had come of it. I couldn't call her a friend but still counted her among the people who might turn a sympathetic ear to the tale of my plight. And this sort of thing was right up her alley.

Susan Fujita belonged to a group practice headquartered at University Hospital. A secretary answered and said that Dr. Fujita was out on the floor, but that she could be beeped. I gave my name and phone number and hung up, wondering what I was going to do in the next couple of minutes, because I felt as if I would have to run from the house, run into the street screaming for anyone to help.

I was about to walk up the walls when the phone rang. It was Susan Fujita.

"Nice to hear from you, Skye."

"You don't know how good it is to hear your voice, Susan."

"Oh? Tell me about it."

I told her. Not about MagicNet or Grant or even Sima Berkowitz, just about walking down the street and getting weird feelings, about my rising anxiety. Strictly symptoms.

At length she said, "Sounds like a panic attack."

"Are they common?"

"Getting more so. This is the age of anxiety, I guess."

"What can be done?"

"A number of things. Therapy, medication, if needed."

"I really don't want to take pills."

"It may not be necessary. What you should do is get in here for observation."

"You mean, check myself into the psychiatric ward."

"In effect, yes. You sound like you need help. I think you want help."

"That's true."

"No stigma attached to coming in for an evaluation. You really sound like an outpatient case to me. But we'll know for sure if you come in. Will you?"

"I guess. Yes, I will."

"Just go to Emergency, tell them I sent you, and we'll do the rest. Okay?"

"Okay."

"Fine. I'll be expecting you. Just get here as fast as you can. Can you drive, or do you think you'll need assistance getting here?"

"I don't drive, but I can walk to University. No problem."

"Fine. You're going to be okay, Skye, believe me."

"If you say so."

"I say so."

"Thanks, Susan."

"You bet, Skye. See you soon."

I hung up and went into the living room and sat down. I lifted the bottle of Corona and drained its dregs, then leaned back and thought. Did I want to commit myself? Was I feeling bad enough to let them lock me up for an indefinite stay? I speculated a while on the way Susan and her colleagues might react to my story of the demon attack, the notion of MagicNet, or Sima's protean house. And what would they think of my habit of talking to dead friends who live inside my computer?

No need to speculate; there was only one way they'd react. They'd toss me into the bouncy cubicle and throw away the key.

Wait a minute, I said. Let's get a few things straight. Do I believe that what happened did indeed happen? I did. Okay, but what exactly happened?

First, Grant got killed by something. He was dead. The police came; they saw that he was dead. They said he was dead. Did I hallucinate the police? No.

Right. Now, had I or had I not talked to some kind of simulacrum of Grant? Did I hallucinate all that conversation?

Maybe. But Sima Berkowitz heard the voice, too. Did I hallucinate her? Maybe. Did I really see her house change its shape and style? Perhaps, perhaps not.

So, taken as a whole, the entire question of my sanity was moot. Perhaps all this crazy stuff had been triggered by the shock of seeing Grant murdered and by my run-in with whoever or whatever it was that killed him. "Posttraumatic stress syndrome." (They used to have simpler names for things. "Shell shock," for instance.) Yes, that was it. Stress. (What the hell does that word mean, anyway? Widely used but almost never defined.) Yes, all this anxiety was the product of stress.

In which case, I should check myself into the local funny factory.

No? Why not?

Because I didn't think I was crazy. Because deep down I thought that everything I'd seen, heard, and been told was real.

I had to talk to someone, all right. And I knew who it was, too.

I got the laptop out of the closet it and set it on the coffee table. I lifted up the screen and hit the 1/0 switch. The screen glowed and displayed the usual prompt, waiting for my command.

I typed "Ouija" and sat back.

"Hey, what's up?"

It was Grant's voice. I realized that I'd forgotten to plug in the voice synthesizer.

"Grant. Sorry I turned you off."

"You always turned me off, kid. Wait, let's drop the levity. You don't look good. What happened?"

I told him.

"Panic attack," Grant said. "Or maybe Merlin working some mojo on you."

"It's possible?"

"Possible. But maybe you just freaked out. Hey, there's a good old sixties phrase."

"Where does Merlin live?"

"In Los Angeles. Studio City, to be exact."

"And his influence can reach here?"

"Through the magical network, yes. Very easily."

"But it occurs to me that the computer was shut off at that point."

"Right. Well, that takes us back to the panic attack hypothesis. Unless . . ."

The computer was silent for a moment.

"What?" I said at last.

"I don't know, but I'm thinking that as time goes on, the less dependent the network is on hardware. On computers. The network might have taken on a life of its own somewhere along the way."

"If that's possible, then Merlin might not need a computer to harass me."

"Could be. But I think computers still figure in, in a big way. I'm sure of that. That's why we have to run Ragnarok."

"Your program."

"Yeah. But I'm not sure we can do it here, in your house."

"No? Why not?"

"Could be dangerous, your being alone like this. That's what happened . . . well, I might as well tell you. That's what I was doing right before Merlin sent his demon after me."

"Oh." I sat up. "Uh, Grant?"

"Yeah?"

"Let's not run that program."

Grant laughed. "I figured you'd have that reaction."

"What do you intend to do, then?"

"Don't know. The program has to be run, that's clear. It might be the answer to our problems. It will definitely give us power enough to rival Jones's. Here's what I think. I think we have to run that program in a place where Jones isn't free to operate. Like, in public. In a shopping mall, on a plane, some place where he can't conjure demons without bringing the mundane world into this."

"He couldn't do anything in public?"

"Maybe not. We have to be sure about that. That's why I have to work on the program a little bit. I didn't build enough protection into it."

"You think that's why he got to you?"

"Yeah. Blindsided me. I didn't think he'd actually conjure something to kill me. Thought he was bluffing. Maybe he was, but he grew desperate, and did it. Hell, maybe he's even sorry he did it. Though I doubt that. I think he's basically a nasty character, underneath."

"So we wait?"

"I think," Grant went on, "that what we should do is hop a plane for California."

"Oh?"

"Yeah. I think Ragnarok will work better the closer we are physically to Jones."

"Why so?"

"The way the network works is strange. Did I tell you that hardly anybody needs to use a modem any more?"

"No, you didn't. How can you avoid using the phone lines? Special lines?"

"In a way. Yeah, magical phone lines. As everyone knows, computers can communicate much more easily if they're directly linked, free of the need for intervening communications protocols."

"Everyone knows that? Okay, I guess I knew that. Go on."

"Well, the analogy holds. If we can get near Jones, we might be able to blow him out of the water, magically speaking."

"Kill him?"

"I'm tempted. Why not? He did me the favor."

I took a long breath. "You're asking me, then, to commit murder. To avenge you."

"No, I wouldn't ask you to do that. I'll do whatever needs to be done. Me. I will be the protagonist, here. I am the shade of Grant Barrington, and I will avenge him. All I'm asking you to do is help get me into position."

"But I'd be an accessory to a crime."

"Ghosts commit crimes?"

I fell silent. He had a point. I thought for a while.

At some length I said, "Okay. I'll do it."

"Good. Just stay with me till I get an opening, a clear shot. Then I will come after him, like black smoke, like a demented giant, and pull him apart nerve by nerve."

I chuckled. "Striking turn of phrase."

"I stole it. No, really, I will take care of that fucking son of a bitch."

"Grant, you have a problem with hostility."

"Shit-can the psychobabble. I mean it."

I nodded. "I think you do."

"Leave mostly everything to me. You get us a plane ticket to LA, pronto."

"My credit's up to the limit."

"Have any cash?"

"After buying plane tickets I won't have any for expenses. I could make a withdrawal from my trust fund." I looked at my watch. "Bank's closed."

"It's not four yet."

"In New York, where the bank and my trust officer are."

"Oh. Well, shit, there must be some way. How much cash do you figure you'll need?"

"Meals, hotel—hell, I don't know. I haven't the foggiest notion what you have in mind . . . Wait a minute. I have another credit card, one I never use. Forgot. I think it's still good."

"Good. Book your flight, we'll worry about the rest later."

"Right." I began to rise.

"Book two seats."

"You need a seat?"

"No, for another person."

"What?"

"You're going to need help."

"Sima?"

"Not Sima. You need someone who understands magic."

"And who might that be?"

"Woman by the name of Jill Lo Bianco."

"Unusual name."

"She's different. Actually, she's a witch."

"Witch, huh." I gave up a groaning, eschatological sigh.

"Pretty, too. But . . . Look, give her a call. Hold off

on the tickets a bit. I have to talk to Jill first."

"Is she MagicNet?"

"Yup. Number's on my disk Here it is."

I memorized the number on the screen and walked to the phone.

7

JILL LO BIANCO KNEW EVERYTHING. SIMA HAD called her.

"Something has to be done," Jill said.

I liked her voice. It was breathy, sensual, rather low. "About Jones?"

"Yes."

"Grant seems to feel there's a need of termination with extreme prejudice. How do you feel about that?"

She didn't answer immediately. "I don't think that's necessary. I'll have to talk to Grant. I really don't know exactly what Grant can do. If that is really Grant you're talking to."

"Have you ever encountered anything on the network like this?"

"Like Grant's ghost? Not ghosts of anyone I knew. Though it sounds a little like what you encounter chatting with Ouija spirits."

"You've done that?"

"Everyone on the Net's experimented with it. You make contact with all sorts of entities. Some just babble, most are noncommittal—but a few are real talkers."

Strange, so very strange, I thought.

"Maybe you'd better come over here and have a chat with this one," I said.

"I will. Where do you live?"

I told her.

Grant's ghost was mostly silent in the interval between Jill's hanging up and her arrival. He said he was working on the program.

I listened to music. I needed something blithe, something lightsome, etched in pristine clarity: Mozart's clarinet concerto. I settled back and listened, focusing my concentration on structure, on the repetition and development of themes.

The soloist was just getting into the final cadenza when the doorbell rang.

Jill Lo Bianco had a face that eluded the word "pretty" but was attractive enough to survive her modishly short hairdo, which she wore like a helmet. Thin but not too thin, she was tall for a woman, but not as tall as I, and I'm not tall, which led me to believe that she simply gave the appearance of being tall. Some people do that. In dress, she favored black: jeans, sweater, athletic shoes, all black, and together with her dark hair they framed and accentuated the paleness of her face. Her dark intelligent eyes emitted heat like a sooty radiator.

We shook hands solemnly at the door, and I had her come in. She followed me into the living room. I pointed to the notebook computer on the coffee table.

She approached the table, stopped, and looked down.

"Grant?"

"Yeah. Hi, Jill. How's it going?"

Jill gave me a skeptical frown before saying, "Grant. Is it really you?"

"It's me. We have a problem on the Net, don't we?"

"Yes." Still looking a bit unsure, Jill sat on the couch. "Merlin's gone bonkers, I think."

"He has a god complex and we have to simplify matters for him."

"Grant, I won't take part in any killing. I realize a great injustice has been done to you—"

"You might call it that."

"—but . . . well, I won't do that kind of thing. You know I'll do anything to defend myself. But I stop short at murder."

"Who said anything about murder? We're going to neutralize Jones. You don't have to murder someone to do that. His influence on the network has to be eliminated. But that means *something* bad's going to have to happen to him. You understand that, don't you?"

Jill gave it some thought. "We can't very well go to the police, can we?"

"No one would believe it. We couldn't prove it. To do so we'd have to take the police into the Net, and that can't be."

I said, "I still don't get that part of it."

"Skye," Grant said, "we're in a separate reality. As time goes on, the Net seems to build up walls around itself, blocking out the reality we know, sealing us off. I'd bet any money that when the state cop investigation is over, they put my murder down to a marauding bear. Or a serial killer. I'd bet they even make an arrest."

I gave a short, deprecatory laugh. "Who will they nab, some homeless grizzly?"

"You know what I mean. The hard part to understand, and I'm not sure I understand it, is that in their world, in the mundane world, it will be true that my murder was done by something nonsupernatural."

I shook my head. "I still don't get it."

68

"Let's work on that. Meanwhile, I want to talk to Jill."

"Sure," I said, moving away. "I'm going to fix something to eat. Jill, would you like something?"

Jill looked at her wristwatch. "Dinnertime coming up. Sure, thank you very much."

I hadn't had a bite all day. Walking into the kitchen, I realized I was ravenous. What to fix that's quick but good?

I don't open cans or thaw TV dinners. If you know a little about cooking you don't need to. I looked in the fridge, found salad fixings, good for starters; also a lemon and an onion, and a few mushrooms. I opened the freezer and saw one lonely package of deboned chicken breasts. Fine. The cupboard yielded a can of tomato sauce, a cannister of flavored bread crumbs, and a box of thin spaghetti. Great.

I popped the chicken into the microwave for a partial thaw, and while that was transpiring opened the can, dumped the sauce into a pan, set it on the stove, and turned on the gas. I added minced garlic, rosemary, thyme, and basil to spice up the bland commercial preparation, then chopped up the mushrooms and onion and threw them in. Quickie sauce. I put on a big pot of water for the pasta.

Cracking the microwave oven door, I palpated the chicken breasts and found them in a semithawed state, just right for cutting into strips, which I did quickly, using a good knife. The strips all got a coat of preflavored bread crumbs. I set a nonstick frying pan on the range and heated it up after layering the bottom with virgin olive oil. When the heat was high, in went the coated chicken fingers, or whatever you want to call them. I added some minced garlic to the oil, though the crumbs were enough to make the chicken flavorful. No such thing as too much garlic—one of the slogans I live by.

Time to put the pasta in and check the sauce. The latter was bubbling away, cooking down just a little. No need to let it sit for hours on the stove; the sauce was thoroughly precooked, though it wasn't the kind of overspiced glop that comes out of a jar, reeking of oregano. It was only lightly seasoned, tailor-made for lazy cooks who like to pretend they're high kitchen but who simply doctor things up.

I flipped the fingers to let them brown on the other side. Taking the lemon, I cut it in half and squeezed juice into the simmering chicken, distributing it evenly all over the pan. Lemon chicken, simple, easy.

While the spaghetti was boiling its way to a not-quite *al dente* state, I prepared a quick salad with romaine and iceberg lettuce, some olives, and a few leftover mushrooms. Soon enough, the spaghetti was done and so was the chicken.

From start to finish, one half hour had elapsed.

I set the table in the kitchen, then popped the cork on a chilled bottle of Frascati. After shoveling the food into serving dishes, I brought everything to the table.

Jill was still talking with the haunted computer as I entered the living room. She looked up.

"Ready," I said.

"Thanks, just a sec."

I went back into the kitchen, sat down at the table and fixed myself a bowl of salad, sprinkling it lightly with a dressing of olive oil, wine vinegar, and garlic. When I was about halfway through the salad Jill came in and sat down.

"Sorry, there was a lot to talk about."

"Hope you don't mind my starting without you. I haven't really eaten since last night."

"Oh, no, go right ahead. This looks great."

By the time I was ready for the chicken and pasta, she had caught up with me.

"This is great sauce. You make this yourself?"

"In a manner of speaking."

"The chicken's great. What is that taste?"

"Lemon."

"Delicious."

"Thank you. Are you convinced you were talking to Grant?"

"Yes. It's uncanny. No computer could know what that one does."

"So it's real? We're in contact with departed spirits?"

"That's about the size of it. Grant wants you to order the plane tickets. I'll pay for mine, of course."

"Fine with me. I take it we're going to LA."

"I guess. Don't know where else we would go, if we're going to do what we have to do."

"I'm still fuzzy on the agenda."

"So am I. But we have to get within striking distance."

"I'm glad you're going along. I was beginning to feel lost in my own private nightmare."

She smiled. I noticed her mouth was small. "Nightmares can be shared, I suppose."

I nodded. "Apparently. You're the second person I know to be involved in this . . . dream. Besides Grant. You and Sima. Are there other MagicNet people in town?"

"A few. Most aren't very active. They lurk."

"Lurk?"

"Sorry, computer slang. They observe. They don't participate."

I decided not to ask what they didn't participate in. "Jill, what do you do?"

"Working on my Ph.D. in education. Speech therapy. You're English Department, aren't you?"

I nodded.

"I was going to take a course of yours, a while back. Conflict."

I nodded again. The chicken was good, but I thought the sauce needed something. Of course. I'd forgotten to add wine.

Jill asked, "You like cooking Italian?"

"My favorite cuisine. Are you all Italian?"

"No, just one side. Mother was Irish."

"I'm thinking you favor your father. The dark half." I gave her a smile.

She hesitated a moment, then said, "Did Grant tell you I was gay?"

"Uh . . ."

Her blurting it out like that puzzled me. Had that smile of mine been interpreted as some sort of overture? Nothing could have been further from my mind. I felt no pangs of arousal whatsoever. The reason wasn't Jill's lack of appeal; I found her attractive, in a strange way. It was simply a matter of my sex drive having gone into neutral since the murder.

These are troubled times. (If you want to have that apothegm cross-stitched and framed for the wall of your den, be my guest.) Both sexes tread lightly, but most of the eggshells are strewn in the path of the male. Perhaps it was always so. Anyway, I had an immediate problem in interpersonal dynamics, if you'll forgive my lapsing into Newspeak. Just how was I supposed to respond to that revelation?

"Oh, that's all right. You're ugly anyway."

Or:

"*Damn! And here I had the hots for you, powerful-like!*"

Or:

"*Hey, no kidding. Do you like cunnilingus or do you just ram your bedmates with a ribbed dildo?*"

Now, any of that is beyond the pale, of course. But what do you say? Do you congratulate the person?—or express solidarity with them in their political struggle? Or do you simply fob them off with a polite "That's nice"? But any of that is fatuous, so there is really nothing to say.

But she had left me an opening, asking only if Grant had told me that she was a lesbian, to which question a simple negative response would be appropriate.

I was about to give that response when she said, "Black Irish."

"Beg your pardon?"

"My mother was Black Irish. They're dark, too."

"Oh. Don't they have blue eyes, though?"

"I think. My mother has green eyes. Like you said, I got most of my genes from my father."

I offered her more wine, which she declined. I certainly needed a refill, though I was still feeling the beer. I didn't want to get drunk but did want to maintain a mild high, enough to ease me through whatever was ahead.

"Are you afraid?" I asked.

"No. I've always been able to take care of myself. And I know the Net. I can handle myself fairly well. Why, are you?"

Okay, I wouldn't admit it either. "No, but I don't know the Net. Maybe you can fill me in as we travel?"

"I'll try. But you have to get a feel for it. Do you know anything about magic?"

"Not much."

"Well, that would help."

"Where does one learn magic?"

"Oh, there are books."

"That you can get at one of the university libraries? Or are we talking about dusty scrolls in ancient crypts, that sort of thing?"

She chuckled. "Magic's no secret. The trick is doing it right. That's where computers come in."

"Yes, so I understand." I took a long drink of wine. "But I don't really understand."

"Actually, it's mostly mental. I don't even run spells anymore. I don't need to. It's like learning to ride a bike."

I nodded a comprehension I did not possess, then rose and took my plate, utensils, and wineglass to the sink, where I rinsed everything off and put them in the dish rack. Jill helped me clear the table. We had the kitchen clean in no time.

"You keep a tidy house," she said. "Me, I live in a perpetual mess."

"I guess I'm just an odd single."

"Huh?"

"One-half of an odd couple. You know, I've never booked plane tickets on short notice. This is going to be interesting."

8

GETTING THE PLANE TICKETS WAS NOT INTEREST-
ing; it was a financial disaster. With no advance notice,
no discounts, no red-eye cut-rate, and no direct flight to
LA from the College Green airport (which consisted of
two cow paths and a wind sock), the best fare the ticket
agent could give me was horrifyingly near four figures.

One way.

I wasn't worried about the trip back. Rather, I was,
but I'd worry about it later.

After putting Jill on the phone to give her credit card
number, I went upstairs to pack. Traveling light seemed
to be the thing to do, so I packed toiletries and one
change of casual clothes. Then I undressed and put on a
pair of black sweatpants that could pass for a better class
of trousers. Over the top went a colorful pullover that
was warm yet looked dressier than the average sweatshirt.
Comfortable yet presentable is the effect I wanted.

"Better keep me running," Grant said when I went
back downstairs.

"Right."

I flattened the screen back and put the compact computer into the carrying bag.

"By the way," I said, "have you figured out why we
don't need the voice synthesizer now? I paid good money
for that contraption."

"Sorry. Don't know, really. But as I said, the longer you're in the Net, the less dependent you become on physical instrumentality. I will admit, though, that things are moving along a lot quicker than they normally do."

"Okay. You'll be all right in there?"

Grant's voice chuckled. "You know, I'm not really *in* the computer."

"Oh. No use asking where you really are, I guess."

" 'They seek him here, they seek him there. Those Frenchies seek him everywhere!' "

I groaned. "Another goddamn cryptic allusion. What is that, *Scaramouche?*"

"*The Scarlet Pimpernel*, you illiterate bumpkin. Are we ready to go?"

Jill was standing by the door.

I said, "We are."

"Then, my friends, let us take that first step."

The first step was driving to Jill's apartment, which turned out to be on the second floor of a commercial building. At street level was a seedy Chinese restaurant, where Jill waitressed part-time, and an empty storefront.

"I'll make it as quick as I can. When's the commuter flight, again?"

"You have fifteen minutes," I told her. "No more."

"Right."

She got out of her battered Subaru, leaving me to sit and think about things, which I did not want to do. The key was not in the ignition, so I couldn't turn it to auxiliary and play the radio, which had nothing to offer anyway but rock and roll and one country music station. There was a paperback on the floor, something with a neologism for a title and a sword-wielding Amazon in a fur bikini on its gaudy cover. I picked it up and began to read. It was awful. Regarding the prose, "purple" was not quite *le mot juste*. I think the actual color shaded into the ultraviolet; and the dialogue was as pulpy as the cheap stock it was printed on. Solecisms abounded; but I continued reading until I heard Jill open the trunk and throw something in.

She got in, started the car, and we were off. She had taken exactly fourteen and a half minutes. The old saw about women taking too long to dress came to mind. Jill was not standard-issue; which is not to say of course that many women aren't, which is *not* to gainsay my life's experience: many are the times that I have sat, scrubbed, dressed, ready to go out, waiting in vain for a woman to get through her interminable toilette. If this be sexism (I am here addressing the ideologue-on-watch), make the most of it.

Traffic is usually not a problem in College Green. Slow trucks on the two-lane highways are, and we got behind one. Jill passed, but we ran up against another lumbering triaxle carrying gravel or some such burden, and now oncoming traffic thickened to prevent our passing.

"If we miss this flight, there's not another out until tomorrow morning," I said.

"We could drive to the city."

"We wouldn't make the connection in time."

"Isn't there more than one direct flight to LA?"

"The eight-forty-five is the last one of all the airlines."

"Maybe we should just get the next flight to O'Hare."

I looked at my watch. "We'll make it."

But did we want to make it?

We made it, and I didn't know whether that was good or bad. We picked up our tickets at the counter but didn't check baggage, then rushed to the "gate" (a door giving out onto a concrete apron) after passing through the airport's security checkpoint. No alarm rang but the woman guard wanted to see the laptop work, so I showed her that it indeed worked, as it was running. She passed me through. Jill was waiting, not having had any trouble.

The plane, a two-engine propeller-driven craft that looked like a flying boat, was in the last seconds of boarding. We ran.

We mounted the rollaway stairs and boarded, and a stewardess showed us to our seats, just forward of the wing on the right side. It was a tiny craft, cramped and conducive of claustrophobia and other private horrors.

But the seats were comfortable. After stowing my valise in the overhead compartment, I took the window seat, as Jill had declined it. I bent over and shoved the carrying bag under the seat in front of me, making sure it was securely wedged in.

I settled back and strapped myself in. Jill did likewise. She had changed into high black boots, I now noticed, and tight black jeans. Her top was mostly black, but had purple designs in it. She wore this outfit well, her legs being long enough for the boots. She had a knack for dressing a tad kinky.

About her neck hung a medium-heavy silver chain, a strange medallion depending from it, positioned squarely between her small, pointy breasts. I was about to ask her about it when the right engine turned over.

It had been a while since I'd flown out of the municipal airport in one of these buckets; I'd quite forgotten how much noise a propeller-driven aircraft makes and how much vibration those huge banging engines and their wildly rotating blades produce. The other engine began to grind and soon the noise was tremendous. Well, to me it was. Jets seem to roar in a whisper, especially the newer, more advanced ones. I suppose in this case it was more the vibration than the noise that distressed me.

After taxiing for what seemed an inordinate time, the plane began its takeoff roll. The speed built to a tremendous rate, more so, it seemed, than a jet's, but I knew this could not be true. The smaller the plane, the closer you are to the ground, therefore the greater the sensation of speed—I guess.

We lifted off the runway and climbed while banking slightly to the left. The sky was clear, and, though it was late in the day, it was still bright. At this time of year, as the sun's path in the sky neared the vernal equinox, there was at least an hour of daylight left. There was, however, a band of purple darkness on the western horizon—an advancing weather front, I thought. Or was it a mountain range? The sudden elevation disoriented me a bit.

"Are you a nervous flyer?" Jill asked.

"Not usually," I said. "Why, do I seem nervous?"

"A little."

"Maybe I am. Tell me something. What do you people do on the Net, exactly?"

"It started out as a network of bulletin boards, like most computer networks. Just endless chatting."

"About . . . ?"

"Magic, New Age, stuff like that. But of course no one ever stays on topic. We talk about anything and everything. And then . . . well, some new software became available."

"Is it true no one knows who created it?"

"At first Merlin denied he created anything. Just improved. Anyway, this stuff came down the line. The first one I played with was the electronic Ouija board."

"The same thing that's allowing us to talk to Grant?"

"I think Grant changed it a lot."

"I see. Okay, what else came down the line?"

"Oh, I downloaded lots of things. A lot of it was new versions of the board software itself. It got to be a lot of fun. It used to take days to get a response to a posted message. With the new versions those responses came quicker, and finally it was instantaneous. We were all on-line in realtime."

"I thought all these networks worked like that."

"You're thinking of the commercial networks, the big ones. Those are run by central mainframe computers. MagicNet is an amateur PC network, run and paid for by dedicated volunteers. There are lots of other nonprofit networks. What Jones and people like Grant did was to boost the system up to the level of the commercial networks. And then they took us far above."

"What happened?"

Jill sat back and stretched her legs. "Things got strange. The software became almost miraculous. Well, it was miraculous. You could actually see the people you were talking to. First, their faces appeared in balloons on the screen. Then . . . then it was as if they were with you. We used to hold meetings at a round table. In a castle."

"Where was the castle?"

Jill shrugged. "In dataspace."

" 'Dataspace'?"

"In the new dimension we were creating. Call it what you want. Cyberspace, virtual reality. But it was more. It was realer than real. Pretty soon, almost anything could happen. You could create any world you wanted. Anything. And walk right into it."

I nodded. "Like Sima's house?"

"Like Sima's house."

"But she said she couldn't do anything with the interior."

"Sima's not gifted, for all she pretends to be. She sticks to basic stuff. Dream partners."

Puzzled, I shook my head.

Jill smiled. "What do you think people started doing with this stuff?"

"Oh. Creating imaginary sexual partners?"

"Sure. That's what virtual reality is really about, don't let anyone kid you."

"And here I thought it was for training astronauts or something."

"Oh, I'm being facetious. Of course it has many noble and useful applications, but the sex part . . . Well, there won't be a sex part, really, until they solve some of the problems that we solved with magic."

"I think I understand."

My gaze was pulled toward the window. I thought I'd seen something out of the corner of my eye, but as I looked out, nothing anomalous presented itself. One wispy cloud floated by.

"You want to know if I did it, don't you?"

I turned back. "Huh?"

"You probably want to know if I did it."

I shrugged elaborately. "If you want to tell me."

"Sure I did. You don't know how difficult it is for a woman to meet other women. I work a lot. I teach, do research, and wait tables every other night and on weekends. The guys have their bars to hang out in."

"Aren't there women's bars?"

"In College Green there's exactly one, and the same people have been hanging out there for years. Not any-one I'm interested in. It's rough. Anyway, yeah, I played around with Dream Lover. It was a fun program—for a while anyway."

"It began to pall?"

"You realize you're not dealing with anyone real."

"But I thought that was the big question."

Jill stared at the ceiling for a moment, ruminating. "I suppose it's not settled. But if all those experiences were with someone real, they couldn't have been human. What was it I made love to? What kind of being?"

"Hey."

The voice had come from the carrying bag. I pulled it out, unzipped it, and took out the computer. I unlatched the service tray on the back of the seat in front of me and lowered it to its horizontal position, resting the computer on it.

"It was lonely in there," Grant said. "Everything okay?"

"Yeah," I said.

"I'm going to find the restroom," Jill said, unbuckling and getting up.

"Are you still nervous?"

I said, "A bit. Still haven't quite recovered from last night."

"I *never* will."

I had to laugh. Gallows humor. Graveyard humor? Otherworldly.

"Have you remembered anything more from that experience?" I asked. "An experience which you say you never had, but . . ."

Again, my gaze was drawn out the window.

"Yes, definite impressions. I know it was a demon. I also know—"

"Jesus Christ!"

"What is it?"

I had seen something unbelievable. It could not have been real.

"Skye?"

I was rubbing my eyes. A cliché, true, but it seemed the thing to do. I looked again. I saw the thing again.

"Skye, what the hell?"

"Can you see? Can you see what's around?"

"I can see to some extent. Matter of wanting to. What do you want me to look at?"

"Look out the window. There's something on the wing of the plane."

"Wait a minute. Oh."

Grant's voice broke into giggling, then into uncontrollable laughter.

"I'm glad you think it's funny."

Grant kept laughing.

"Jesus Christ," I complained. "Even if it's funny, it's not *that* fucking funny."

"Oh, Christ, Jones has a sense of humor, that I'll give him. Don't you remember the movie remake they made of it?"

"What movie remake?"

"Of the original TV episode?"

"The original TV—?"

I got it. Yes, I remembered, vaguely.

"He's really whacking that engine, isn't he?"

I looked. Yes, "he" was, if it was a he. Are gremlins sexed? I didn't know.

"Are you sure it's Jones who's doing this?"

"Well, do you believe in gremlins?"

"I believe in the demon who did you in, so why the fuck not gremlins, or elves, or purple-and-green striped unicorns, for Christ's sake."

"Take it easy. Jones is trying to psych you out."

"He's doing it."

"Don't let him."

"I guess no one else on the plane can see that."

"No one but Jill."

"You think Jill will see it?"

"No telling. She may, depending on—"

"What can I see?" Jill wanted to know as she sat back down.

I gestured out the window. She looked.

She broke up.

"I'm glad you both think this is a laugh riot we're having," I said, feeling an emotion as rare and as strange as the apparition out on the wing of the plane.

The emotion was stark terror mixed with extreme annoyance.

9

W E WATCHED THE STRANGE CREATURE GO TO work on the engine with a sledgehammer. It was not unlike watching a motion picture in which live action and animation have been blended. The creature itself, a dwarfish anthropoid with feral characteristics and pronounced sociopathic tendencies, was a meld of several familiar cartoon characters.

In time the engine began to belch plumes of black smoke. Before long it burst into flame. The creature laughed. I could hear it. Then, brazenly making a face at us, it hopped off the wing and dropped out of sight.

I watched as the engine was slowly absorbed by an expanding fireball. I looked at Jill, who to my astonishment was flipping through the in-flight magazine.

"Doesn't this concern you in the least?"

She glanced out the window. "I sort of logged off the system temporarily."

"Can't you see what's happening?"

"It's not happening, Skye," Grant said.

"Excuse me," I said.

Jill swung her legs out of the way as I sidled out. I walked forward down the aisle and found the stewardess, a middle-aged woman with henna-colored hair, sitting in the first seat on the right.

"Pardon me, but is the pilot aware of what's going on with the starboard engine?"

Startled, she leaned over the adjacent seat and peered out the tiny window. "What's wrong?" she asked anxiously.

"Can't you see it?"

She craned her head back and forth. "No, what?"

"Look at the engine!"

"I'm looking at it, sir. What's the problem?"

I took a deep breath. She turned and stared at me, confused, frowning suspiciously.

I said, "You don't see it, do you? Never mind, I must have been mistaken."

"Sir, what am I supposed to be seeing? Sir, what—?"

After sitting back down I looked out again. The engine was completely engulfed and the flames had spread to the wing. Suddenly I could see an incongruity that had not registered before. The flames danced almost straight up. I had no idea what the plane's speed was, but knew that it was enough to blow the flame almost to invisibility and reduce the smoke to a thin blue trail. Whatever the nature of this phenomenon I was witnessing, it wasn't real. Rather, it was some sort of projection ineptly superimposed over what *was* real. This conclusion hit me like a bucket of cold water—a shock, but bracing and somehow soothing.

Grant said, "Are you convinced that we're being kidded?"

"Yes."

"Are you convinced the plane won't crash?"

"Yes."

"And that we'll be okay?"

"No."

"Well, two out of three . . ."

"Jesus Christ," I said quietly.

"What?"

"The wing just exploded. Falling off."

"That's nice."

I said, "Grant, listen. I understand that this is a message. But consider the content."

"I'm hip. Yeah, he's a nasty son of a bitch. We knew that."

"This is a warning. What I want to know is, can he follow through on his threat?"

"What threat?"

"To crash the plane, of course!"

"Keep your voice down. He wouldn't do that. As for the possibility of his harming you in another way, look at what he did to me. But now we've got protection. I've been working really hard at improving Ragnarok. And I've beefed up the system software to the point where I don't think Jones can muster anything to go up against it."

"Whatever you say." I sat and stewed, and eventually thought of something. "What are we going to do when we get to LA?"

"Nothing, tonight. You're going to hole up with a friend of Jill's."

"Another denizen of the Net?"

"No," Jill said. "That would be dangerous. We have to seek neutral ground."

I gave up and sat back. The plane had no engine now and lacked a wing; but it didn't matter, because it really wasn't missing a wing, not really, and that engine was working at the peak of mechanical efficiency. Everything was fine now. No kidding.

*   *   *

When the plane's wheels screeched against the runway and I felt the earth under me once again, relief washed over me like floodwaters from a ruptured dam.

It was a quiet night at the big airport. Departing flights were few; or perhaps their roar went unheard because I was temporarily deaf. The flux of passengers was thin, though, and I concluded that my eyes, though they had recently been deceived, corroborated my ears.

There was time to kill after we picked up our tickets at the desk and went through the security checkpoint, where I was asked to demonstrate the laptop once again. I watched Jill run her huge bag through the X-ray conveyor device and suddenly wondered why she wanted to lug that big thing around. Maybe it was the only piece of luggage she owned. Knowing that you shouldn't run a computer through x rays (because it does what?—demagnetizes them?—I suppose), I took Grant's electronic apartment (I thought of him as living in there) out of its bag and proffered it to the guard.

"Neat little things, these," the man said admiringly. "How much?"

"With plastic money, who cares?"

He chuckled and passed me through.

I was still recovering from our bogus air disaster. I had looked out of the window immediately before we landed. The wing had rematerialized, ditto the engine, which seemed in tip-top mechanical condition.

So, we sat and waited for our flight to begin boarding.

"You said something about our staying with a friend in LA?"

"I'm going to call him right now. He's usually in. If he's out of town, though, we'll just have to risk a hotel."

"Jones won't want to cause trouble for us with non-Net people around?"

"That's the idea. Of course . . ." Jill frowned thoughtfully.

"What?"

"I can't predict what he'll do. We know he's capable of taking extreme measures." She let out a long breath. "I still have trouble believing it."

"I don't," I said. "I saw it."

"I'd better make that call."

She got up and walked off. Gaze drifting to the right, I noticed a distinguished-looking man, of perhaps fifty years or so, sitting two maroon molded-fiberglass seats away. He wore a long woolen overcoat and a broad-brimmed fedora, both black. Longish hair, stark white, corn silk white, crawled down the back of his neck. There was something odd about the face, something theatrical, exaggerated. It looked heavily made-up; or it might have been that he was extraordinarily handsome in a theatrical way. He sat with his legs casually crossed, reading a newspaper.

He looked at me and smiled. His eyes were ethereally blue, stratospherically blue, two small disks of skylight, sun, and cirrus clouds, the high, cool vastness above the earth. Another theatrical affectation. No one's eyes could be that blue. Colored contact lenses? I stared at him, nonplussed.

"Evening," he said, and went back to reading.

I continued to stare at him. His shoes were like black mirrors. His face was pale, almost colorless, perhaps slightly green—but that could have been because of

I could only stare back at him. His eyes seemed to have changed color. I saw fire in them, and smoke, and wreckage strewn across the countryside.

"It must be the awfulest way to die there is," he went on. "The agonizing drop as you sit there helplessly, the ground rushing up. Then, the titanic impact as tons and tons of metal burrow into the earth. And you're in the middle of all of that. Oh, it's quick, that I'll grant, but in those few seconds, even in that last split second, there is an eternity of pain and terror. Think about that. Dwell on it."

He smiled, and the strange light in his eyes died. Then he turned and walked off.

In my entire life I had never been in an emotional state such that I desperately needed alcohol—until that very moment. Memory is the discontinuous thread that binds us together. I don't remember any particulars of the transition, but the next thing I saw in front of me was a shot glass full of whiskey. I picked it up and drank it down.

I looked about. I was sitting on a chair at a bar. The bar was in the airport terminal, I was fairly sure. I had walked in from the concourse.

"Skye?"

I looked behind me. "Huh?"

"Another, sir?"

I turned. It was the bartender, a young man with a lot of brown wavy hair.

"I'm sorry?"

"Would you like a refill, sir?"

I looked down at the shot glass and realized that I never drank whiskey neat. "Another, please, on the rocks this time."

"Yes, sir."

In fact, I almost never drink whiskey; but now I needed it.

"Skye."

There was that voice again. Oh. Grant's voice. Then I noticed that the carrying bag lay on the chair to my left.

"What?" I said.

"Finally! I've been trying to get your attention for the last five minutes."

"I was preoccupied."

"I'll say you were, listening to that hokey hallucination. I was yelling at you, telling you to ignore it. Didn't you hear me?"

"No."

Grant sighed. "Jesus Christ. I guess Jones really got to you."

"I'm not getting on that plane."

"Okay, I think I can understand that. But it's the same as the gremlin, Skye. No real reality there."

I shut up until the bartender brought the drink and went back to the end of the bar.

" 'Real reality.' Interesting concatenation of words."

"You know what I mean. It's just another empty threat."

"Did Jones make threats before he killed you?"

Grant's voice made no reply.

"Ah," I said with perverse satisfaction. I took a long sip of blended and possibly watered whiskey. It had no kick at all.

"Jill's probably looking for you," Grant said.

"Let her. Let her get on the plane if she wants to."

"She's hardly going to leave without you. She'll be worried, Skye."

"Let her worry. Sorry, but I don't feel much like talking. Now, would you kindly shut the fuck up and leave me alone?"

"No problem."

10

"**Y**OU REALLY SHOULDN'T TREAT JILL THAT WAY."

"I said shut up."

The bartender stopped pretending he wasn't watching me, and stared.

"Sorry," I called to him. "I just had a fight with my wife and I'm upset as hell. So damn upset I'm talking to myself. My apologies."

The bartender shook his head, grinning wryly. "Can't live with 'em, can't live without 'em."

"That's the truth."

"You sure you're okay, sir?"

"Yeah, I'm fine. I'll be shoving off in a minute."

"Take your time, sir."

"Thanks, uh . . . ?

"Call me Tom."

"Thanks, Tom."

"Sure."

Presently Tom exited through a swinging door that seemed to lead back to a storeroom.

"Skye, please go back to the gate."

"No. I will not get on that plane."

"There's nothing to worry about. Trust me."

"Who the hell was that guy?"

"Who the hell knows? Some phantom Jones conjured up."

"Phantom, eh? Looked real enough to me."

"Oh, the Net can be very real, if you go along with it. Just remember, if you don't like what's happening, you log off. You pull the plug. You get out."

"Why didn't you do that when the bogeyman attacked?"

"No time. He caught me by surprise."

"I don't know how to pull the plug. I don't know anything about the Net. Every time I ask you anything about it you answer in ciphers. Fuck you."

"Skye, pull yourself together."

"I am together. I want to avoid being pulled apart limb from limb. Or getting my throat eaten out, thank you. And by the way, fuck you."

"Skye, grow up."

"You tell me to grow up, then you blather on about a magic network, some cockeyed mass delusion that's a cross between a nightmare and Disneyland, and you expect me to believe all this shit. You can go to hell."

"I'm there, pal. I'm there."

"Skye?"

A new voice. I turned toward it, and saw Jill walk into the bar.

"The plane's boarding," she informed me.

"Fine."

"I was looking all over. If I hadn't glanced in here as I walked by—Listen, why on earth did you run off?"

"Jones spooked him again," Grant supplied.

"Oh." Jill seated herself sideways on a bar chair. "Was it bad?"

"Oh, hell, no," I said. "Just some weird guy telling me the plane would crash."

"Bullshit." She looked off, scowling. "He was lying."

"Yeah, so I'm told. Some ghost told me. O lost, and by the wind grieved, ghost, get the hell away from me."

"That's insensitive," Grant said. "Ghosts are the most aggrieved minority of all."

"To hell with them."

"As I said, I'm there."

"This is all about drugs, isn't it?"

Jill shot me an odd look and said, "Huh?"

"All this, some gang scuffle about drugs. You people are involved in drug dealing."

"Close," Grant said.

"Close, my ass. That weird guy was real, and so was the guy that killed you, Grant. That was no demon, nor a bear neither. You got whacked by the mob."

"Skye, you know better than that."

"No, I don't. There's lots of it going around these days. Random violence, drive-by shootings. All related to drugs. Drugs, the curse of the second half of the twentieth century and the embodiment of the *Zeitgeist*. Speaking of ghosts."

"You're wrong, Skye," Grant said.

"I hope. No, wait. I hope I'm right. The alternative is more than I can handle. Either way, I'm out of it."

I upended my drink and took it down in a gulp. A piece of ice hit my nose as it tumbled out of the glass and onto the bar. My grand gestures always invite the risible. Tom came out from the storeroom and I ordered another drink.

When the drink came and Tom had retreated to the storeroom again Grant said, "When I said 'close' I meant it. Jones is involved in something."

"Drugs?"

"No. Computer crime."

"Of course. How do you know?"

"His life-style is upscale and he has no visible means of support. He says he has a consulting business, but that of course means nothing."

"Okay, so he's a computer criminal. No skin off my nose."

"The public inevitably pays the price. You know that."

"Okay, I know that. What can I do about it?"

"Get evidence and get it to the authorities."

"Uh-huh." I shrugged.

"We can't pin my murder on him, but we can put him away. Hard time. He's probably filched millions by now."

"A job for the police, surely."

"Jones is smart, he's slippery. Good chance he might get away with everything, including murder."

I sighed out a black cloud of rue. "Oh, for Christ's sake."

Jill got off her stool and came over to me, got close, her right breast pressing against my upper arm.

"You've got to help us," she said.

Oh, now what was this? A promise of something she wouldn't think of delivering?

"But why do you need me?" I asked petulantly. "I don't know anything about any sort of hocus-pocus and I know next to nothing about the Net."

"That's what's protecting us," Grant said.

"Huh?"

"I'll explain later. Here comes the bartender."

Jill's firm breast kept its pressure against my triceps. It felt good there. Damn it, she was indeed attractive. Even that awful *nouvelle* hairdo added to it. Maybe lesbians aren't really interested in other women, only in exercising control over men; because there is something in lesbianism that heterosexual males find paradoxically attractive. They are at once aroused and repelled, achingly envious yet approvingly voyeuristic. The lesbian knows this and can use it to advantage. I leave it to the deconstructionists of gender to parse this tangled sexual syntax in all its convoluted perversity (if you'll pardon).

Jill asked sweetly, "You will help us, won't you?"

"Oh, shit." The black cloud turned a gray shade of resignation. I pushed my glass away. "Right. Let's go."

Once again through the security gazebo, same routine.

And into the plane. Once in my seat, I was almost petrified with fear. As the plane taxied, I was seized with an impulse to run down the aisle screaming; I wanted to burst into the cockpit with a gun and threaten to shoot out the instrument panel if they didn't stop the plane and let me off. But it was all I could do to move a muscle.

Then the wide-bodied jet roared down the runway and threw itself at the dark sky and there was no chance of my getting off. No chance at all, except when my body flew from the wreckage in six directions at once, ragged smoking shards arching from the fireball to litter some desolate hayfield.

But the aircraft kept climbing and city lights dropped away and behind until darkness overtook the land.

The sky glowed with moonlight that made clouds look like specters, angels of death hovering over a doomed kingdom.

I sat back and tried to control my breathing. The fear had turned to a numbness, lack of any feeling at all. But I could move again, and when the overhead warnings blinked out I unbuckled and got up to find the restroom.

The big plane was filled about half. Business people, this lot, taking a late flight back to the home office, along with the odd undergraduate or retired off-season vacationer. I walked unsteadily along the aisle, casting glances to either side, not wanting to meet eyes but on the lookout for anyone suspicious—for anyone who looked to have a nasty message for me. Not that I would do that person harm, killing the messenger being the most egregious of gestures. No, I would simply avoid that messenger. But none here looked the part: no theatrical affectations, no strange costume, no stagy manner.

The toilet reeked of disinfectant and stale urine seeped into cracks. I sat and voided, not trusting myself to direct an accurate stream from a standing position; I then rose, hitched up, and washed. I looked in the mirror and saw a haggard face. My beard looked scruffy, and the areas where it was trimmed badly needed a shave. I resolved to get rid of the beard when the chance arose. I dislike a beard in the warm weather. I had grown one because beards protect against icy winds and I had the walking habit. College Green's winters were of Pleistocene intensity and duration. With regret I noted my glacially receding hairline. My teeth had endured neglect today, or so it appeared. Incipient pimple there along the left cheek? A triviality, really, what with the universe coming apart at the seams.

I splashed more cold water on my face and paper-toweled it dry. Refreshed but not completely regenerated, I opened the door and stepped out.

And there, before me, was a green elk, lounging in its seat and paging through a copy of *Paris Match*.

I thought it was an elk. The green was an iridescent shade that clashed violently with the creature's purple pin-striped suit. An open briefcase lay on the service tray of the empty seat beside it.

I let out a groan. "What the hell did I do to deserve this?" I muttered, asking no one in particular.

The elk turned its great antlered head and replied, "You mean, what have you done lately?"

I stared at it. The thing shrugged and went back to reading.

Shaking my head wearily, I walked back to my seat. I tried not to acknowledge additional monstrosities among the other passengers.

"Have you noticed anything?" I asked Jill after sitting down.

"Yes, out the window."

"Huh?"

I looked. There were strange lights in the sky, swooping and cavorting. Some of them drew near, and I could see they were various things: parti-colored birds, lantern-bright; fireballs of every hue; strange figures all aglow. One of them looked to be a witch on a broomstick.

"What is it?" I finally said.

"Oh, hard to say. Stuff in the ether."

"What ether?"

"The MagicNet ether," Grant said from his mobile digs, which lay at my feet. "Random phenomena, origin unknown."

"Not Jones again?"

"Probably not. Feel better now?"

"A little. Do we get dinner on this flight? For some reason I'm hungry."

"Dinner *and* a movie," Jill said. "It's a sci-fi feature."

"Splendid, just what I need."

11

OUR FLIGHT CONTINUED WITHOUT INCIDENT; THAT is, without any incident that could be said to have occurred in the world of everyday experience. Outside the plane, aloft in the icy stratosphere, lights flitted, shapes took form, then grew faint and amorphous; phantasmagoria came into existence and ceased to be within a matter of seconds. Some apparitions were longer-lived. Sitting in my comfortable seat, I was treated to a light show, a surreal animated movie, or—looking at it another way—a display of bizarre weather phenomena, all for the price of the plane ticket. No extra charge. The aurora borealis kept us company most of the way, fluttering and shimmering over everything like a silk veil afire. At least I thought it was the aurora.

Inside the plane the situation grew passing strange. Humanoid animals of every description appeared, occupying empty seats. Some, I do think, supplanted human occupants, but that is not certain. The human passengers paid them no attention whatsoever. What sorts of animals? Oh, moose, elk, zebra, wildebeest, bison, elephant—these were a bright traditional pink, except for one cyan nonconformist—and some I couldn't identify.

Jill, absorbed in a genre paperback, ignored everything. Grant was quiet. I watched, noted, tallied, alternating my observations between window and interior.

I watched golden flowers with fimbrillate petals bloom in the sky over a landscape of phosphorescent lakes. Next, a multicolored chessboard pattern appeared, forming a vast plateau in the sky. That faded quickly, giving way to a geometric plane on which masses of raw color swirled; this happened while, above, swarms of golden insects moved across the face of the moon. (That's to be taken literally. The moon did indeed have a face and it looked a bit like that of my friend in the black overcoat and fedora. Then the features changed to something resembling Winston Churchill's. Or perhaps it was Jackie Gleason's.) I witnessed numerous other phantasms, most too strange to describe.

After a time I grew weary of the show and sat back. "Grant?"

"Yo."

"You never explained."

"Explained what?"

"Why I'm your protection."

"Oh. Well, it's like this, and it relates to what I said before about the Net being very insular. You're outside the Net. Rather, you were, and now you're a part of it, though still somewhat of an interloper. Thing is, and I guess this sounds silliest of all, you don't quite believe in the Net."

I nodded. "True. Actually, I think Susan Fujita is right and I need a weekend at University Psych."

"See? You doubt. And that is why . . . how shall I put this? Jones's power over you is limited. Learning how to handle you is taking up a lot of his time and energy, and Jill and I are benefiting from that."

"His power over me is limited? But he's causing me no end of mental pain."

"Yeah, but he can't do much else besides."

"That's enough."

"Not much else for now, anyway. Until you become a full-fledged Net person. Don't ask me how that comes about."

"Do I have to be a full-fledged computer nerd?"

"No. You simply have to be able to run applications, and you can do that."

"I'm computer-semiliterate. Let me couch it in other terms. You're breezing through the complete works of Immanuel Kant—whereas, for me, reading a supermarket tabloid is a major undertaking."

"I catch your drift. Yeah, that's true. All the more reason that Jones has trouble affecting you."

"Let me get something straight about Jones. You're saying he's the all-powerful god of this little universe? Omniscient, too, I take it. He knows when the sparrow falls?"

"Well, he's the reigning demiurge. And, yes, he knows his bird droppings. It's just that in this little microcosm, you need the right stuff, and he has it more than anybody. So far. He's the fastest gun—switching metaphors. But some new young shootist could ride into town any day, call him out, and gun him down. You never know."

"That's more or less what we're doing, isn't it? Calling him out."

" 'Fraid so. It's going to be another gunfight at the O.K. Corral. But fought with software."

"I get the feeling I'm in *High Noon*." I looked at Jill. "Except I feel more like Grace Kelly than Gary Cooper."

Jill laughed.

"Again," Grant went on, "let me qualify all of the above by saying that in the end the Net might not have much to do with computers at all. You're seeing that the hardware aspect of this is fading. The extent to which this is happening surprises even me. We must be pushing on to the next phase of things."

"Then what's it all about, Grant?"

"I don't really know. It would be just a guess on my part. We may have made contact with a different realm of existence. With another universe, maybe. Or, as I said initially, we may have created a new universe."

"Interesting notions, all of them. And not a little frightening."

"Certainly. Anything totally new is frightening. But it could mark a change in the way the human race perceives the nature of reality. I tend toward the creation theory, myself. I think what's happened is that the global computer and communications net has taken on a life of its own and turned sentient."

"Another interesting if improbable notion," I said.

"Yeah, but I don't think it's so improbable."

I looked out again. The light show seemed to have faded to a degree. There were dabs of color glimmering here and about, but not much else. Reticulated patterns of light appeared on the ground, but these looked mundane—city streets, connecting highways, and so on.

By any chance, were the weird passengers fading as well? I rose from my seat a bit and peeked. A magenta gazelle winked at me.

Nope.

They served dinner, which I ate without tasting; the movie I watched but cannot even recall the title, much less the plot. I ordered three stiff drinks, drank them down in rapid succession, then cranked my seat back. After a few minutes of watching an interesting multicolored guilloche pattern march across the sky, I went to sleep.

I dozed fitfully for what seemed like hours, and in reality was. I dreamed chaotically, but when I awoke retained nothing but the aftertaste of emotional residue. There was both fear and wonder, along with surprise, and terror. There was an intense feeling of strangeness.

I looked out. Below lay a vast skein of light spreading out to the horizon. Nothing phantasmagorical this time: this had to be the Los Angeles basin at night. Our wide-body whispered over the neon glitter, the tawdry glamor, the mansions and the swimming pools, the squalor of the slums and barrios, the miles and miles of sunbaked concrete—in short, the entire gridlocked urban neoplasm in its all-pervasive metastasis. Looking at it for the first time, I liked it, enjoyed watching it roll by. It seemed endless.

The plane banked, glided, banked again, aligning itself along its electronic corridor in the sky. It slowed and seemed almost to hover; but then the ground came up fast and rooftops raced by: we were still traveling at a terrific clip. Suddenly, the urban sprawl fell away and we were over the runway.

The huge plane touched down with a solid thump, and relief shot like an opiate through my body. I went limp. I almost cried.

Jill looked at me, smiled, then calmly marked her place in her book and put it in her small carry-on bag. She sat back, unbuckled, and crossed her legs.

I exhaled noisily. "Jesus," I said.

"You see? Nothing to worry about."

"I see now. But what about all the crazy—?"

I craned my neck, looked around, unbuckled, rose, and looked again. No puce moose, no chartreuse elk— no Day-Glo Shriners or Odd Fellows for that matter. No cartoon animals, no craziness. Everything was normal. I slid back down into my seat.

"All the crazy what?"

"Oh, nothing. Nothing at all."

Jill's grin was sly.

I laughed an ironic, inward laugh. At myself mostly. At the lunatic world I lived in and the nuttier one in which I was vacationing (briefly, it was to be hoped).

I suddenly remembered something. "Jill, ye gods, I never asked if you reached your friend."

"I did. He said he'd put us up."

"Who is he? What part of LA is he in?"

"Harlan Ellison. Lives in Sherman Oaks."

"Is it far from the airport?"

"Oh, up the San Diego Freeway to the Valley, and then up Beverly Glen. Not really far by LA standards."

"What's he do?"

"He's a writer."

"Movies?"

"TV, mostly. But he's well-known for his fiction, too. Fantasy."

"Should I have heard of him?"

"Of course."

I wasn't well-read in genre fiction, not out of snobbery but because I'd always rather preferred nonfiction and poetry to most fiction. I will admit to being probably the worst-read English professor in academia; and, believe me, that is saying something.

Not that I haven't trudged through novel after dreary contemporary "serious" novel, looking for some clue as to why the author wrote it, why he felt it necessary that his readers get down on all fours, for the six hundredth time, to view the dark underside of American life as exposed in all its invidiousness by the light of his (usually academic) hero's tender sensibilities and penetrating critical intelligence. What amazes me is that for these startling revelations, applause is always expected. Never mind that it had been done to death by 1948 . . .

Never mind.

It was a little after ten o'clock, and the night air was cool, but somehow you could tell that it had been a warm day. Back East it was still winter. Here, by comparison, was a perpetual tropical paradise, except when it monsooned for a few weeks and rained torrentially. Before flash flood control, the downpours washed palatial houses off the hillsides and into the canyons. Now they simply wiped out trailer parks out in the flats.

Brushfire, mudslide, flash flood, high seas, riots every other decade, and let us not forget earthquake: six reasons why no one should want to move to the Los Angeles area. Yet still immigrants come in human waves. En masse, the human being is not a rational animal. However, I speak as an outsider. The Angelenos I've met merely laugh at the notion that their city is a dangerous place, quite aside from the usual social dysfunctionalism which most great cities share.

We deplaned and retrieved our luggage. I was about to suggest that we take to our destination one of those multi-passenger limousine vans, of the kind that of late have sprung up to serve most airports, when Jill told me that she had reserved a rental car.

"The old saw about a car's being vital in LA is trite but true."

I nodded. "I should have thought of it."

"Well, you were preoccupied."

The rental agency ran a twenty-four-hour desk. Jill signed, picked up the keys, and we headed out into the vast parking lot, or one of them. Each of the agencies had its own area, marked off with signs (or "signage," to use a recent and shameful nonce word). After a short search we found our car, a Japanese subcompact, dark blue with a gray interior: perfectly adequate for our purposes, whatever they were. (I was still mostly in the dark regarding this matter.) We loaded up the trunk and got in, me with the precious and damnable carrying bag still in hand.

Los Angeles rolled by at ground level, and I watched. The freeways were as advertised, as wide as rivers and thick with traffic. It was murderous. But our trip wasn't long. We drove north until the freeway threaded up through a notch in a range of steep mountains—the Santa Monicas, Jill told me—and down into the San Fernando Valley. We exited onto Ventura Boulevard.

Not knowing LA, I got lost from that point. Jill, I now learned, was a native Angelena, hailing from Torrance, wherever that may be. In fact, her parents still lived in southern California, near San Diego.

Eventually we turned right off Ventura and began to climb, passing through residential fastnesses, strongholds of families which grew increasingly patrician with each increment of elevation. I guessed that this wasn't the height of the socioeconomic scale; everybody knows Bel Air and Beverly Hills are the ne plus ultra; but I also knew that LA real estate was as pricey as hell and that it must cost a pretty penny to live in this area.

We climbed up into a canyon, the road switching back and forth. Lots of traffic here, too. Traffic everywhere,

here in LA, where the internal combustion engine is almost a life-form.

I looked out the back window. The valley now began to look as LA did from the plane, an electric sprawl, a grid. A net. There seemed to be any number of discrete urban centers out there in the flats, all linked by endless suburbs, all lit up like Christmas.

We turned off the canyon road and descended again, passing houses to either side of the narrow, winding road.

"There's a shortcut to Harlan's house but I forget it," Jill said. "This is the long way, though you do get to see some stuff. How do you like the place so far?"

"Like all great cities, it has a character all its own," I said, "and it's evident even at first glance."

"You're right. Still scared?"

"No," I said, maybe with a hint of annoyance.

She sensed it. "I wasn't taunting you. Sorry."

"No, it's okay. I was jittery and still am. I wish I took drugs."

"You threw down a few drinks. Didn't those help?"

"That was hours ago, and I didn't feel them then."

12

*H*ARLAN ELLISON'S HOUSE STOOD ON A LOT FRONT-
ing a steep grade. I could see immediately that the place
was unusual. Something was going on with the imposing
facade, a mass of earth tone stucco, but not much detail
revealed itself in the darkness. Jill parked down the hill
from the recessed entrance.

"Nice of your friend to put us up."

"He always has guests and it drives him crazy. No,
you don't understand, Harlan loves to be driven crazy.
He loves people."

"Don't like the idea of putting him out."

"Don't worry. He's like a Jewish mother. 'No, stay,
stay. Make yourself at home, take all the silverware, I'll
just lock myself in a closet.' And then for some strange
reason you feel guilty if you *don't* stay."

"I think you'll be safe with him," Grant said. "Ellison
is a celebrity, and Merlin Jones isn't going to be mucking
about here."

His voice sounded more disembodied now—Not "disembodied." Well, there's no good word for it *Discom-
puterized?* In other words, the voice now seemed less
connected to or associated with the computer than it
had at any time previous.

"You've been quiet," I commented.

"Been working. This is not going to be as easy as I thought. The situation constantly changes."

"Oh? Which means what?"

"You might have to give me a little more time."

"I have other friends in town," Jill said. "I don't think there's going to be a problem about a place to stay."

"Yeah, but any delay plays into Jones's hands. Can't be helped, though."

"He respected and even feared you, a little."

"Hey, you're talking about me as if I were dead."

Jill laughed. The laugh went against the grain of her usual sober mien. It was a silly, giggly sort of laugh. I would have laid odds that she was at constant pains to keep it under control. One's laugh can give one away. In her case, I wondered what would be revealed.

I asked, "Grant, do you know Harlan Ellison?"

"Read his books, saw him at a few of his appearances, but never got to know him. He's not network, anyway, so we can't really talk."

I mulled that over as we got out of the car and began to climb the hill. In passing, I noted that the stucco bore much arcana in both inscription and bas-relief. I didn't stop to study it all.

The entrance court was well lighted, less so the carport off to the right, where one subcompact was parked. I looked up. Gargoyles along the roof line. Not filched from Notre Dame, but originals, it appeared. Standing before us, the front door was a work of art in itself, a construct of unusual wood pieces skillfully fitted together into a rectangular collage.

Jill rang the doorbell while I continued to take in what was for me the exotic ambience. The air in southern California is different, and by that I don't mean the pollution. Quite apart from the chemical additives, and perhaps even in spite of them, it has a certain balmy softness not found elsewhere.

The artful front door opened and within its frame appeared a compact man with thick gray hair offset by a perennially boyish face. Dressed in mauve T-shirt, lime Spandex shorts, and baby blue running shoes, the sight of him evinced in me a nanosecond-long flashback of our bizarre but colorful airline flight. Seeing us, he smiled broadly. He seemed jovial, distracted, enthusiastic, annoyed, harried, and warmly benevolent, all in one energetic *Gestalt.*

"You made it! Get in here."

We entered, and Jill embraced him. "I'm glad you're up."

"Yeah, I'm up. I got twelve fuckin' people up in my office and I can't get 'em out. Those fuckers can't take a hint."

"Harlan, this is Skye King."

Harlan Ellison looked at me, eyes dilating with genuine wonder. "Skye . . . King?"

"Uh, yeah."

His face suddenly changed expression and he raised a cautionary finger. "You don't even want me to mention it, do you? You're sick to death of people doing the inevitable number on you."

I shrugged. "Frankly, well—"

"With a name like that I could have been a star." He extended a hand and we shook. "Glad to meet you, Skye."

"Same here."

"So what's the occasion?" Ellison asked, turning to Jill. "Not that you need an occasion."

"Oh, just some traveling. Spring break."

"It's spring back East?"

"Just about."

"Hell, it's been spring here since February. I keep telling you Eastern types to move out here but, Christ, you're a stoic lot. Suffering is good for the soul! Well, suffer, what do I give a shit. Hey, look, I've got to move those people out up there, so why don't you two sort of—" He made expansive gestures. "—fade into that part of the house. The kitchen, yeah, the kitchen—"

"Anybody up there I know?" Jill asked.

"I don't know. You know Jay Szymanski, don't you?"

"We talk on one of the computer networks."

Ellison scowled. "Is everybody wired into those goddamn idiot circuits? I mean, does *everybody* have their cranium soldered to a computer all day?"

"It's a new form of group consciousness," Jill said. "You ought to join us, Harlan."

"Group consciousness. Jesus Christ, sometimes I get the feeling I'm in *Invasion of the* fucking *Body Snatchers!*"

Ellison assumed a zombie pose, arms extended, and stalked around the foyer. "Join us, Harlan! You'll realize what you're missing when you join us . . . jooooiinnn us . . ." He did a good imitation of a theremin, the electronic musical instrument that was the workhorse of the sound tracks of nineteen-fifties B sci-fi flicks.

Jill giggled through the performance.

Ellison quit clowning and shook his head wearily. "Honest to God, I don't know what's happening to people."

"It's the global village," I said. "McLuhan's curse."

"You got that right. Curse of the networking nerds."

Jill said, "Oh, come on, it's just a way of communicating. Don't be such a Luddite."

"A *happy* Luddite. They oughta bring back Western Union telegrams, with the kid on the bike, you tip him a nickel, and that's your communication. Anyway, come on up, if you want to."

"Sure. Skye?"

"Uh, actually . . ."

"Okay, Skye, be unsociable, what do we care. Come on, Jill."

"Skye, are you sure?" Jill looked unsure herself.

"No, go ahead. The trip really wiped me out."

I walked with them to a door that was impossibly small. A truncated oval, it was under four feet high. Ellison opened it, and the sound of laughter drifted out.

"Skye, just make yourself at home," Ellison said, then stooped and went through.

"You'll be okay?" Jill asked.

"Sure. Have fun. Uh, that door . . ."

"I don't think you've ever been in a house quite like this one. Go explore."

"I might."

"I'll be right out. Just want to say hello to some people."

"Sure."

Jill bent over and, Alice-like, passed through to Wonderland. I went into a crouch and peered in. I could see a pool table surrounded by what looked like a huge library and an amazing collection of bric-a-brac.

The amazing collection wasn't contained by that single room. It practically overwhelmed the house. I had never seen a more heterogeneous, idiosyncratic, and comprehensive collection of objets d'art in my life. It was nothing less than astonishing. There was a distinct emphasis on American consumer culture—soda bottles, cigarette tins, commercial art, neon signs—but this genre by no means comprised the bulk of the miscellany. There was simply everything here, from movie props and gumball machines to scrimshaw and original works of art.

I roamed the labyrinthian house. Aside from the unending display of stuff, there were more books than some public libraries have, books of all sorts and in all categories and on all subjects, though genre fiction seemed a trifle overrepresented. One encountered masses of shelving at every turn.

On the walls hung oil paintings, watercolors, prints, silkscreens, posters . . . even colorful cartoon "cels" from famous animated films. Enthralled, I studied these and other movie memorabilia: the house's Hollywood character asserted itself in no uncertain terms.

At long last I went into the kitchen, into which the collection also had spilled. I slid into a horseshoe-shaped breakfast nook and gazed out the back window. There was nothing behind the house but an expanse of brush-covered hillside mounting to a high ridge.

I saw nothing strange out there, for which I thanked whatever forces of good there were in this universe—or for that matter any other universe. I sat staring at this tiny patch of unspoiled southern California wilderness until I heard voices in the foyer singing a chorus of good-nights.

Then Harlan came in with Jill and another woman: Harlan's wife, Susan, to whom I was introduced. Petite and blond and attractive, she had an English middle-class accent, if I knew my British accents—which I did not.

Susan shook my hand. "Very nice to meet you, Skye. Harlan, I'm exhausted."

"Go ahead, I'll be with you in a minute. I'll bed these folks down."

"I can stay up if you want. I'm always good for a second wind."

"No, sweetheart, you go ahead. I will not keep you waiting, my queen."

Susan feigned hauteur. "Just . . . 'queen'?"

Ellison dropped to his knees. "You're my *goddess*!"

Susan laid a divine hand on his head. "You may rise. Call me Ishtar."

Ellison rose. "Yes, Ishtar. Can I call you 'Ishy'?"

"Well, okay, but 'Ishy-poo-honey-pie-snookums' is right out."

Ellsion kissed his wife. "Run along, She-Who-Must."

"Okay. Jill, sorry, but—"

"That's okay, Susan," Jill said as she perched at the edge of the horseshoe-shaped seat. "Get some rest; we'll talk in the morning."

"Good night." Susan left the kitchen.

Ellison slid into the other side of the nook. "So, are you still writing?" he asked Jill.

"Haven't had time. I work, go to school. It's been crazy."

"Too bad, you wrote some good stuff."

"I'll get back to it." Jill added for my benefit, "I met Harlan at a writing workshop he taught at."

"Teach?" Ellison said. "You can't teach writing."

"Helped out at," Jill amended.

"You read piles and piles of horrible shit, but every once in a while you find a nugget in all the dross, and it's worthwhile. When was the last time you submitted anything?"

"Oh, been so long I forget. Still working on a novel. It's the work of Sisyphus."

"Short stories are where the real action is, esthetically speaking," Ellison said. "I'm sick of overblown books that take forever to build. If you can say it in seven pages instead of seven hundred, you're a craftsman, not a hod carrier on some vast construction project."

"Oh, I like novels. Big thick ones, too."

"So do I," Ellison said. "If the thickness is justified. I'm not saying you can cover life and love and war and peace in a short story the way Tolstoy did in his epics. But you can make the same points, and you can make art just as well if not better."

Jill turned to me. "Skye, do you write?"

"A few inept attempts at fiction. Poetry's my main crotchet, I'm afraid."

"Craftsmanship there, too," Ellison said. "Listen, we turn in early around here, usually, and it's late, and it's been a rough night. I'm going to fade away. Jill, you've been here, you know where the guest rooms are."

"Uh, we're only going to need one."

"Hey, whatever. There's a daybed, there's a couch, you can crash on the floor, you can go camp in the back. But watch out for rattlers."

"The guest room will be fine," Jill said. "Thanks, Harlan, we really appreciate it."

"Are you guys hungry? I'm not going to cook for you at this hour, but you're welcome to raid the refrigerator. There's cold cuts, pizza-fixings—let's see, I think there's leftover moo goo gai pan in there."

Jill looked at me. "Skye, are you hungry?"

I shook my head.

"No, thanks," Jill said, "we're fine."

"You're sure? I don't want you should go to bed hungry. Anything I can get you?"

"No, Harlan, go to bed."

"I will do that. I will. Have a good night, people."

When Ellison had gone off, I turned again and looked out the window. There was so much light outside that I thought a partial moon must be up, but then realized that the starless sky was aglow with city light. There is no real night in LA.

"Is he always solicitous about his friends' welfare?"

"Always. I told you, there's a bit of the Jewish mother in him."

"He has quite a place here."

Then Jill said, "Did you see all of it? You ought—"

I said, "What's the matter?"

"We forgot the luggage. Damn, I bet the security system is on."

"You go tell Harlan to disconnect, I'll go out. Just give me the car keys."

"Are you sure?"

"Sure, I'm sure."

"Okay."

Jill handed over the keys, slid out of the nook and left the kitchen.

Presently, I wandered into the foyer. A tiny red light shone above the front door. I watched it until it turned green. I heard a click. Taking that as a cue, I tried the door. It opened, and I went out, leaving the door ajar.

This was a quiet neighborhood, a good way up into the hills, well above the bustle of the valley, the lights of which I could see from the street. These were the LA boondocks, which few outsiders know. I had not been aware that you could get a feeling of being out in the sticks right smack in the middle of Los Angeles. Thank God for mountains; otherwise LA would be a one-dimensional urban mass, and less interesting (not to say more brutal) for that.

Neighboring houses were dark. I walked down to the car, opened the trunk, and took out our suitcases. The trunk was lighted and I checked for anything we might have left. I had parked the computer on the dining room table. There was nothing else. I pushed the lid of the trunk down.

He was standing beside the car on the curb, smiling at me, dressed in an ice-cream suit, pale green shirt, white tie, and a tropical hat with a pastel yellow hatband. A large pink carnation graced his lapel. His corn silk hair seemed longer.

I jumped a foot straight up. His approach had been totally silent, and I hadn't spotted any movement, though that suit would have lit up the shadows. I had no idea how he had appeared there.

"Sorry I startled you."

"No, you're not, you bastard!" My heart was pounding.

He chuckled. "You're a bit jumpy. Well, in truth, the danger's not passed. In fact, it's just beginning. Let me tell you something straightforwardly. You ought to drive back to the airport and get the next flight home. You really should."

"I just might, you son of a bitch."

"I'm very glad to hear it."

"Look," I said. "There are laws against stalking people, against harassment."

He turned his head slightly and arched one eyebrow. "Oh, are there?"

"Yes."

He shrugged. "And what if there are?"

"Leave me alone. Stop accosting me."

"If it's against the law to stand in the street engaging someone in idle but pleasant conversation, I'm unaware of it. But if that's the case, our society is in a sorry state of disrepair."

"It's against the law to threaten somebody, on the street or off."

"You're alluding to our meeting earlier this evening? I was merely voicing a neurotic fear I have, a fear of flying. It helps to act out my worst fantasies. Sorry you were the unwilling cotherapist. Didn't mean to cause you trauma."

"You just got through traumatizing me again. Look, get the hell away from me, or I'll call the police."

He chuckled. "How do you know I don't live around here? Why, that fine house across the street may be mine. You, sir, might be the interloper. It might be you who is stalking me."

"That won't work," I said. "We're guests here."

He looked the house over. "Fine place, if a bit *recherché*. He's a celebrity? Movies, I take it."

"A writer," I said, wondering why I was telling him anything. Foolish to do so.

"Ah, reminds me of the one about the silly starlet. Heard that one?"

"Look, if you think I am in any sort of mood—"

"She was so dumb she slept with the writer."

"Very funny, Mr. Jones." I picked up the bags and started back up the hill.

"That isn't one of my names. Well, good night to you. Get some rest, you might need it come morning."

"Asshole," I muttered.

"Sorry?"

"Good night!"

"Ah, yes. Good night."

Jill was waiting at the door.

"Were you talking to someone?"

"Yeah, Merlin Jones."

"Merlin? But that's impossible."

"Why?"

She began to answer but stopped and looked over my shoulder.

Hearing footsteps behind me, I turned.

We were both surprised when a bathrobed and moccasin-shod Ellison jogged into the court bearing a strange-looking pistol that, at first blush, I took to be a toy. With its telescopic sight and flaring, futuristic lines, it looked like something out of *Star Wars*.

"Where'd he go?" Ellison wanted to know.

"You heard?" I asked.

"There's a one-way window in that wall that I use as a lookout for vandals," Ellison said, "fan weasels with ideas about chipping away part of the frieze out there. The vent was open, and I heard you, but I didn't hear who you were talking to. Who was it?"

"Don't really know," I said. "Some nutty guy. He's been following us, making a pest of himself. Saw him last at the airport. He may live around here."

"I doubt it. Christ, he was fast. I heard you, got the gist real quick, and I grabbed this cannon from under the bed and tore out the side door and came around. But all I saw was you going up the hill." Ellison walked back to the road and looked out. "Did you see where he went?"

I followed him and looked. I shook my head. "No."

Scanning the semidarkness, Ellison seemed annoyed, even disappointed. "Well, I'm going to sleep with this baby loaded and proximate."

"That's a curious piece," I said. "I've never seen bolt action on a pistol."

"It's unique, packs the wallop of a high-powered rifle. It's a true pistol-rifle. I've used it hunting wild boar in the Sierra Madres."

"What make?"

"It's called a Remington XP-100. Fires a .221 Fireball cartridge." He reached into the side pocket of his blue terrycloth robe and brought out a wicked-looking rifle round about 3½ inches long. "These. And the scope's a Bushnell."

"Looks like one deadly weapon," I said.

"It surely is, my friend."

We walked back through the court. Jill let us in and closed the door.

In the foyer, Ellison confronted both of us. "Are you guys in some kind of trouble? Tell me, I got connections. I can help."

Jill shook her head. "It's nothing, Harlan. Really. Just a nut."

He looked me in the eye, then her. "Yeah." He shrugged. "Okay, you don't have to tell me."

"Harlan, you and Susan are in no danger. I wouldn't have come if I'd thought that."

"Listen, trouble around here is nothing new. Once had a sniper up on the hill in back. I've had vandals, people walking in here. One time . . ." Ellison broke into a yawn, fought it off. "Never mind. This is a dangerous world." He yawned again. "Excuse me. Oh, hell. Good night again, people. Keep your powder dry."

When our host had gone, Jill gave me a perplexed look.

"It was Jones," I said.

"Jones? How do you know?"

"It had to be. Who else is involved in this?"

"No one that I know of."

"Have you ever seen Merlin Jones?"

"Only on the Net."

"So you know what he looks like?"

"Yeah, more or less. Early on I think he appeared as he really is. But as time went on he liked to dress up his image. What did this guy look like?"

I described him and asked, "Was it Jones?"

"Doesn't sound like him, but as I said, he can change his appearance . . ." Looking off, Jill worried her lip between her teeth.

"Think of something?"

"Huh? No, nothing. Let's go to bed."

She said it casually. However, I had no illusions about the nature of the sleeping arrangement—I gathered ours was to be a chaste bed. On the other hand, I was too distracted, worried, and upset to take advantage of the invitation had it been a sexual one.

"I hope you don't mind our sharing a bed," she said. "I don't think we should be separated. We'll sleep better, too. I know I will."

"Right, it's a good idea."

She apparently didn't think ruling out other possibilities was necessary.

The room was small, or might have looked so because of all the stuff, for here, too, was unbelievable clutter. I might point out that it wasn't messy clutter. In fact, each item looked scrupulously positioned. Everything was in its place.

I stripped to my shorts and turned down the covers on the double bed. I got in. The sheets felt clean, smooth, silky.

The encounter with Jones, or whoever he had been, had affected me more than I realized. I began to shake.

The lights went out. Jill got in and sensed something was wrong. She put a cool hand on my heaving chest.

"Are you all right?"

"I will be in a moment."

She rubbed my chest soothingly. "Was it bad?"

"He gives me the creeps. Jill, who the hell is he?"

"I don't know. Wish I did."

"Could it be Jones?"

Jill took some time answering. "It might be."

I listened. Nothing. The house was quiet.

"Skye?"

"Yeah."

"I'm afraid, too."

"That doesn't make me feel better. Makes me feel worse."

"Sorry."

"God, I'm tired."

"Me, too."

I rolled to my side. Jill aligned her body against mine; it felt good to be touching someone. The bed warmed, and I melted into sleep.

13

I WOKE UP AND STARED AT THE CEILING, TRYING TO focus an amnesiac fog of uncertainty, to shed the anomie of being unable to recall where I was and how I had come to be there. At length the answers resolved to something resembling clarity, and I didn't like them, not one bit.

I sat up and saw that Jill was gone. I rose from the bed and got dressed, then looked at myself in the mirror of the inlaid dresser (a very nice piece, one of many in the house). The Dorian Gray syndrome continued apace, with me playing the part of the portrait. I left the room.

The sun was not up, but the sky was turning a ghostly gray. Looking for anybody, I searched dark hallways and odd-shaped rooms, encountering more oniomaniacal clutter: more valuable art, more artifacts, more curiosities, statuary, sculptures, paintings, collages, toys, pewter figurines, model airplanes, carved chess sets, Chinese martial arts paraphernalia—and of course books, books, books. Not to mention records, and tapes, and CDs, and . . .

"Skye!"

Jill came running out of a corridor I hadn't noticed before. She looked out of breath.

"What's wrong?" I asked.

"Harlan and Susan. They're not here."

"Could they have left early?"

"Not without telling us."

"Some emergency?"

"They would have let us know. Besides, their bed hasn't been slept in."

"So? They made it before they left. And are you sure they have only one bedroom?"

"Look, I've been here many times, and they're not in the house, believe me."

"Jogging?"

"Harlan hates that."

"Good man. But, surely—"

"Skye, I just have this funny feeling."

I decided it was no use challenging her conviction that something was amiss. She had me persuaded. "What do you want to do?"

"Leave. I don't want to involve them."

"I thought the whole idea of coming here—"

"I don't know what's going on, Skye, but I think we should leave, now."

"Okay, fine."

"Where's Grant?"

"The computer? Shit, I left it on the dining room table. Shouldn't have done that."

We ran to the dining room and were relieved to find the carrying bag still on it. The computer was inside, and still running. I wondered how long the batteries could possibly last.

"Grant?"

The voice spoke. "Yeah, hi. I started to run Ragnarok."

I took a deep breath. "Can that account for—? Well,

I don't even know what's wrong. Jill's convinced that Harlan and Susan have disappeared."

"Interesting. They probably didn't disappear. I think what might have happened is this. Another major overlay has come down, a new layer of reality."

"Meaning what?" Jill asked.

"Meaning that the world has changed for us, but not necessarily for Ellison and his wife."

"Changed for us," I repeated. "I don't understand."

"Neither do I. They might be waking up this morning to find you two have flown the coop. Vanished."

"Are you saying Jill and I have doppelgängers somewhere, in some other universe?"

"Possibly. You might look at it that way. In some universe, I might still be alive. My death may have only happened on MagicNet."

"All right, I'm beginning to have some idea what you might be driving at."

In truth, I had only the vaguest notion of what he was driving at.

Grant went on, "But maybe we shouldn't think of it in scientific terms—'alternate universes' or some such notion. Better to say that MagicNet's reality is interwoven with the so-called real world."

"But how can we get back into the main warp and woof?" I asked, adding, "So to speak."

"Not sure we can, right now. Later, maybe. Once we get this thing resolved, everything might revert to normal. You might come back here and find the Ellisons alive and well, going about their daily business. And having no memory of your coming in the first place. Hard to tell what the final situation might be like."

"What should we do now?" Jill asked.

"Get in the car and drive over to Studio City. Get

as close as you can to Jones's house."

"Sounds easy enough."

"I don't think it's going to be easy," Grant said. "There are obviously a lot of reality changes going on."

I swallowed hard. "Obviously."

We left the house. Jill made sure to leave the place in a secure state, activating the various alarm devices. How she figured it all out, I don't know.

"Want me to drive?" I asked.

"No, I'll drive."

That was fine with me. I am a terrible driver and hate driving, having learned only the barest rudiments of the art long ago. I maintain my driver's license only because one dare not, in this technophilic civilization, do without a driver's license. One simply *cannot* do without it.

Jill had told me that Ellison had a small staff of helpers who minded the store when he was away, but they didn't show themselves. There was no one in the street, and no cars either, which I thought a mite unusual. After all, this was a weekday in Los Angeles.

Jill started the car and we rolled down the hill. I looked up at the slopes, which were covered with dead grass overgrown with what I took to be sagebrush, though I was not sure. I knew next to nothing of the flora of the West in general or "SoCal" in particular. I couldn't tell mesquite from a mosquito, nor piñon from pine; and the notion of a cactus had always struck me as a noxious botanical improbability. Those nasty, prickly things really don't exist save in B westerns.

If Ellison was a happy Luddite, I was a content Easterner, glad to live in a climate that delivered four distinct seasons, along with lots of rain to provide enough water for some decent vegetation. I like my trees plentiful and my grass green and growing. In the East, aside from an occasional dry spell, there is no anxiety about the water table running dry. Here, civil wars could erupt over water rights.

The road wound downhill, then up again. Houses got scarcer the farther we drove.

"Do you know Jones's address?" I asked.

"I've looked on the map, and the street's just off Ventura. That kind of worries me."

"Why?"

"Because he brags about his place a lot, how nice it is, and if that's true, he should be farther up the mountain, where property is more expensive and you get the view."

"Maybe he lies a lot."

Jill lifted her broad shoulders.

The sun had risen blood-red in the east, hanging low over the mountains. It looked strange, too.

Jill made a series of lefts and rights. The terrain looked even more desolate now, parched and dry, beige and brown mottled with gray-green. But most of LA has that look most of the year, or so I'm told: beige grass dying under the struggling scrub. But now even the scrub looked sere.

We seemed to have left the residential areas. I couldn't see any houses and there were no business sections either. There wasn't much of anything.

We drove on for some time. I was completely lost. We had started out on the side of a mountain, but now things seemed to have changed. We had either reached the ridge or gotten ourselves into a spacious canyon.

"I don't recognize this, and I've been up in these hills

a lot," Jill said. "Must've made the wrong turn."

"Does it always look like this?"

"Sort of. Well, not really. Actually this looks a lot like what's up in the high desert, around, oh, Palmdale. See those rocks?"

"They look familiar."

"Oh, Jesus."

"What?"

"That looks like Vasquez Rocks."

"What's Vasquez Rocks?"

"It's a county park now, but it used to be a favorite movie location. They've shot thousands of westerns there. In fact I think it's still used as a location."

"Oh, yeah. You mean those uplifted strata? I recognize them. What's the problem?"

"Well, the problem is that Vasquez is about fifty miles north of LA. What in the world is it doing here?"

"I'll bite."

Jill looked worried. "I don't have an answer."

"Oh. I was rather hoping you did."

We came to the end of the asphalt and hit dirt road with a bump. The road dipped as it threaded between two massive boulders, then wound to the right, heading toward the rocks, which I now realized had, in addition to westerns, provided the backdrop for more than one sci-fi movie or TV drama, although I would have been hard-pressed to name anything specific. The place was picturesque in a Saturday-morning action serial sort of way. Above it all the sky was a serene Technicolor blue.

"Seems we took a shortcut," Jill said, stopping the car. "But how the hell did it happen?"

I had no answer. I checked the rear, then looked off on my side. Rocky hills seemed to go on and on. No houses in the area, no people, no campers, though it did look to be a great place to camp. If you don't mind having to check your boots in the morning for vipers, scorpions, and assorted premiums.

"I'm stumped," Jill said. "Something is definitely happening."

"What do you suggest?"

Jill ruminated as the engine idled. "I think we should turn back."

"Good idea."

"No place to turn around here."

She rolled the car down between the boulders and up a low rise. Here the road widened a bit. Jill ran the car up an embankment, then began maneuvering, backing and filling.

It was a tight space, but she managed expertly.

"Thank God for rack-and-pinion steering," she said. "And small Japanese cars with tight turning radiuses."

"There are some fine American cars with all those things," I said patriotically.

"Yeah."

We headed back up the road but encountered no asphalt. Jill drove on and on, clouds of ocher dust rising in the car's wake.

"Wasn't this where the paving ended?"

I shrugged. "I thought it was just up the road."

Jill drove about a quarter mile before stopping. She put the gear stick in park and sat back, exhaled.

"So much for going back the way we came. Weird."

"Weird, yes."

"It happened so quickly," she said fretfully. "I can't figure out how I got lost."

"I don't think you got lost," I said. "Somebody lost us, or wanted us to get lost."

133

Jill nodded. "You're right. It's Merlin." She looked to the rear. "Well, he wanted us to head toward the rocks. Maybe we should."

"Why?"

"Get Grant out."

"Huh? Oh."

I reached inside the carrying bag and took out the computer. The screen was blank. I tested the batteries. They were dead.

"No computer."

"Damn."

"I should have recharged it last night. Didn't think of it."

Jill gave me an admonishing glare, her brow lowered. "I wish you had."

"Sorry. I don't know much about computers, especially this type."

She looked off and made an effort to get control of her breathing. "I shouldn't get on your case. You really don't belong in all of this."

"He does now. Hi, guys, I'm still here."

It was Grant's voice. It still seemed remotely connected with the computer, but the etheric tether was composed of but a few strands.

"How are you operating?" I asked.

"Oh, we've gone beyond mere electricity. Ragnarok has run. Now it has to fight it out with Merlin's stuff. Both are on the network's hard disk. Put quotes around that last."

"Virtual hardware," Jill said.

"Yeah, that's the concept. We're creating something between technology and magic, a meld of the two. MagicNet is really a nonmaterial construct, the first in human history."

"You could say that mathematics is a nonmaterial construct," I countered.

"Call it a nonmaterial artifact. Call it what you will, it's unprecedented."

Jill asked. "What should we do now, Grant?"

"Keep driving. Merlin's playing games with you, and will likely continue to do so for a while."

I asked, "Then what?"

"If Ragnarok's successful, then Merlin's power will be gone. He'll be finished on MagicNet. He might even die in the process. Hopefully, he will."

"Who's hopeful, you or he?"

Grant laughed. "English professor to the core. Okay, let me rephrase that. It is to be hoped that Merlin won't survive the change from one software system to the other."

"That must be one powerful program you ran."

"It was," Grant said. "I did my best. It also helped that I can actually perceive MagicNet as a totality, and Merlin can't. Merlin's a wizard, but still mortal. I can see in several dimensions. It takes about eleven to hold MagicNet in its entirety."

I began an attempt to digest this morsel of thought-food as Jill urged the car forward again. Our destination was a mystery to me, but I felt disinclined to ask. Does it matter which way you go in an imaginary landscape?

It wasn't long before I saw what looked like an intersecting road up ahead. It had the look of leading to something; a decent highway, perhaps.

It was then that the car's engine died, utterly giving out. We slowly rolled to a stop.

Jill turned the key in the ignition. A feeble clicking came from the engine. She tried again, same reaction.

She sat back and seemed to relax. Looking at herself

in the rearview mirror, she ran both hands through her short dark hair, plumping it up, smoothing it, preening it. Thus refreshed and rededicated, she tried the ignition again.

Click.

"Shit!" Jill gave the steering wheel a vicious thump with her fist, then fell back in her seat as if she were exhausted.

I looked out. Strangely enough, the sun was going down. Stranger still, it was going down very fast.

In no time, as if reality had become a movie run at high speed, night fell and a pale moon rose.

"This is crazy," Jill said.

I nodded agreement.

14

*J*ILL TRIED THE STARTER AGAIN, WITH THE SAME RE-
sults. All that sounded beneath the Toyota's hood
was a pathetic rattle.

"It's completely dead," Jill said, disbelieving. "But it
was running fine, no problems."

The night was quiet but for the forlorn chirp of one
or two crickets, if they were crickets. (Was this the
season for crickets in southern California? Couldn't be,
I thought. Maybe they weren't crickets.)

I said, "What should we do?" and then added, "You
know, that question seems to repeat a lot."

Jill turned a knob on the car's radio. We heard no
sound, not even static.

"I don't know," she said. "I don't think we ought to
get out and walk. God knows where we really are."

"Are we anywhere? You as much as said that the route
we took was geographically impossible."

"Maybe we're still in LA, and just think we're out at
Vasquez Rocks. That make sense to you?"

I nodded. "Some. If the gremlin on the wing was
just an illusion—or shared delusion, or whatever—then
maybe what we're seeing out here—"

I interrupted myself to focus my hearing on something

that had crossed its threshold: the sound of leaden footfalls, along with another sound: heavy, labored breathing.

Jill stiffened, hearing it too. The sounds seemed to be approaching us from the front, and I could only imagine their being produced by some great shambling thing that plodded and stumped, dragging ponderous feet, its breath a wheezing gasp.

In other circumstances I would have thought the sound comic, an effect dubbed from a B-movie sound track, more than appropriate to the setting around us; and it was true that behind my fear was a vague, giddy hope that this was all a practical joke of Byzantine complexity, years in the making, just now coming to fruition. I would sit helplessly as the payoff neared, the rasp of its ragged breath filling my ears. But it would turn out to be a guy in a clown suit who would release a riot of pastel balloons and shoot confetti out of his ears.

A joke, perhaps. Yet in my wildly fibrillating heart I truly believed that something wicked this way was coming.

"Jesus Christ," Jill said.

A few yards in front of the car, a hulking shape took form in the moonlight. I did not spend much time trying to discern its finer features. Jill and I were out our respective doors and running before it took another step.

We ran along the road. The moon peeked over oblique strata ahead, silhouetting their raked alienness. Moonlight limned boulders like giant morels to either hand, and the wash of its diffuse light scrubbed the sky clean of stars except for a very bright few. Their configurations seemed unorthodox, alien as well. This

was another planet, and some inhuman beast was in
pursuit.

189 EXT. NIGHT—ALIEN PLANET   189

Our hero and his [scratch that]. Our heroine
and her swain are pursued by the monster.
They run, he trips and falls. [A trope of chase
scenes.]

> SHE
> (helping him up)
> Are you all right?

> HE
> (grimacing)
> Think I twisted my ankle.

They both look back.

190 INSERT—ANGLE ON ALIEN   190

as the monster relentlessly plods toward
them. It is dark but we can see the creature's
great taloned feet trampling the dust.

191 BACK TO SCENE   191

They react. She points to the hills.

> SHE
> We can hide in the rocks!

They dash off, she in the lead. He follows, looking exhausted and not a little craven.

192 INSERT—EXTREME CLOSE UP   192

A hideous V-shaped mouth, dripping foamy green fluid . . .

And so forth.

We did take to the hills, following a rabbit path that wound among the boulders. If this were a western, we would now choose strategic cover, pull out our six-shooters, and commence holding off the posse. Unfortunately, whoever the producer of this movie was, he did not supply his actors with props appropriate to either genre, sci-fi or "oater" (as the show-biz trade papers call horse epics). We had nothing but the semidarkness on our side, if darkness were a factor at all. I myself took it for granted that aliens could see at night.

We ducked behind a tablelike mass of weathered limestone and peered over it, down the hill. We saw nothing, but still heard the breathing and the shuffling and the plodding. Perhaps I had the genre wrong entirely. The thing chasing us could easily have been a werewolf instead of an alien.

Similar, perhaps, to the one that had killed Grant. The same one, perhaps.

The thought made me realize I'd left the computer in the car. No matter, it was dead; and on my personal horizon of expectations, death was now a looming possibility.

The sound seemed to be advancing steadily up the hill toward us, following our trail.

"Shit," Jill muttered. "It's probably a phony, just like everything else, but we can't take the chance."

"Right, Grant took a chance, and look where it got him."

"It got me here, Skye," said a familiar voice behind me, "right in the soup with you."

I whirled and fell on my buttocks. And there stood Grant—lanky, semibald, paunchy Grant in longish hair, scruffy clothes, and thick glasses; it was either him or a simulacrum accurate to the large mole on his left cheek. It convincingly reproduced Grant's general air of not caring about his appearance, nor caring much, really, about anything, an attitude one readily deduced from a glance at him. Whichever case obtained—real Grant or ersatz—he appeared neither distressed nor very dead. In fact, he looked very much alive.

"Grant!" Jill got up and hugged him. "What's going on?"

"If all this business was some kind of joke," I said, picking myself up out of the dust and gravel, "and you faked your death and everything else, rest assured you are going to be one dead son of a bitch very soon."

"I'm dead, I'm dead," Grant said in mock fear. "Please don't kill me!"

"Then would you please tell me what in blue blazes—"

"Magic," Grant said simply. "I'm a ghost; you're seeing a ghost. What's so amazing about that?"

"Nothing, I guess."

Grant flashed a toothy smile. "So, how have you guys been?"

Although I was glad Grant was . . . if not alive, then *undead*, and although we were still friends and everything, in truth I felt like throwing a rock at him.

I said, "Just peachy keen, thank you very much."

I sidestepped to get a view down the moonlit hillside. Something was moving among the rocks, tending generally uphill. I still couldn't make out what it was, but whatever it was, I had no desire to tangle with it, Grant or no Grant.

"We'd better get the hell out of here," I said.

"Oh, that thing could cause trouble if you got close to it," Grant said. "But you'll notice that it isn't very fast. It's a movie monster."

He had touched upon a truth. Movie monsters never move fast, yet they invariably and quite paradoxically catch their prey, who, as often as not, sprint like startled deer.

"Follow me," Grant told us, then appended, "He said, as if he knew where the hell he was going."

He led us up to the ridge and down the other side of the hill, dodging boulders left and right, then set us to following a path twining through an immense jagged formation. I tripped several times but didn't fall; a good thing, for if I had, I would have doubtless cracked a shinbone.

We loped downward. The rabbit trail took its time getting anywhere, switching us forth and back. Around us, silent and shadowy in the moonlight, the alien landscape phlegmatically served as a backdrop for this chase scene out of *The Three Stooges Meet the Wolf Man*. It did not laugh at us. It did not care.

We came out from the rocks to reach the bottom of a gully through which ran another road—or the same one swung around the mountain to meet us; I did not know. On the other side of the road the land rose to foothills of rubble that climbed halfway up the face of a sheer cliff.

As we came out onto the road, I heard the sound of

a motor coming from somewhere on the plateau high above.

"Someone else is here?" Jill wondered.

Headlights appeared along the edge of the cliff and leaped out into space, falling, the automobile they belonged to slowly going end-over-end. With a horrendous crash, the car hit the mound of talus at the base of the cliff, rolled down it, and ended up on its roof near the road.

We ran to it. As we neared, I could see that it was a blue Toyota.

It was our car.

And there, a bloody mass of shattered bone and matted hair, trying desperately to crawl out a window, was I. My features were quite discernible in the pale, liquid light.

The rear of the car flashed into flame. In no time the entire car was engulfed, a pyre of melting plastic and blistering paint, throwing up gouts of ugly black smoke. Screams commenced. It sounded like Jill's voice. I squatted and looked. She, or her duplicate, was trapped in there, too.

Jill kneeled beside me and stared in disbelief, horrified and yet somehow fascinated. "Oh, my God."

"Don't pay it any mind," Grant scoffed. "Merlin, honest to God, you fucking don't know when to quit."

We watched our doppelgängers burn to death. The screams were quite convincing.

"What's it mean, Grant?" Jill finally asked.

Grant shrugged. "Could mean that in the real Los Angeles, you crashed and burned."

"But we're still alive," I said. "Here. Wherever 'here' is."

"Yes. But I doubt that's what happened. This is just

Merlin's gentle way of telling you to slow down. Although I'm kind of puzzled why he'd be concerned with you now, now that the damage has been done."

"Unless there's more damage to be done," I said.

Grant scratched his ever-present three-day growth of beard. "Yeah. Maybe. We're in unknown territory. No telling what's going to happen."

Gradually the fire burned itself out. Then, as Jill and I watched in stupefaction, our blackened skeletons crawled out of the carbonized husk of the car, got up, and did a dance.

"Thanks, folks!" one of them said, waving a phthisic arm.

The other waved, too. "Love ya! Goo'night!"

Doing a snappy sidestep, they exited stage right. When they reached the berm of the road, both osteological vaudevillians collapsed to piles of bones.

Grant chuckled. "Does that answer your question?"

"What question are you answering?" I said.

The sun rose very quickly, impossibly fast; like an immense skyrocket it rose, bursting into a fireball that blinded us.

15

W E WALKED ALONG THE ROAD WITH OUR PAL
Grant, the friendly ghost. The fierce sun was merciless,
heating the rocks like lumps of pumice in a gas barbecue
grill. The heat broiled us. I speak for Jill and myself;
Grant seemed cool and collected.

Buzzards, or what I took to be some species of scav-
enger, circled overhead. I had never seen Death Valley,
but our surroundings looked the part: lunar desolation,
rocks and dust, little else. The air was drier than a dead
prospector's bleached bones.

"So, just what was the the import of that little vaude-
ville act?" I wanted to know. "Does it mean that in some
version of reality, some strange universe somewhere, Jill
and I are dead?"

"You guys can go home," Grant said, as if I had not
spoken. "Get to the airport, take the first plane out."

I chuckled. "Might one ask where the airport is in
this wasteland?"

"Oh, I have a feeling . . ." Grant stopped and pointed
ahead.

I looked toward the next bend in the road and saw
a glint of color. We walked a bit farther and saw that
it was our Toyota Corolla, quite undamaged, stalled in

the middle of the road as we had left it, both doors still wide open.

"You see?" Grant said. "You've been had."

The three of us got in. Even with ventilation the inside of the car was like an oven. Jill yelped when she touched the sun-heated steering wheel. Grant took the backseat and began fiddling with the laptop.

"A little juice left," he said, and I could see that he had something on the screen, which puzzled me. I had been sure those batteries were as dead as he was.

Jill tried the ignition, and the engine turned over and started with no difficulty. She looked at me and shrugged, and I returned the gesture. She put the transmission in gear and started us off down the road.

The terrain had changed again, I noticed, and again I couldn't say exactly when it had changed. Now it looked less arid and more Angelean, which is to say semiarid and like unto a movie set where it was not bland and undistinguished. Were we phasing through different realities again?

We were indeed. Now the lay of the land took on some aspects of the terrain immediately about the Ellison residence.

"This looks like Mulholland," Jill said.

Which I knew to be a street or road in LA.

"Damn it."

I looked back at Grant, whose gray eyes (I asked myself, Were his eyes always that color?) still stared at the laptop's small screen. He was typing quickly and expertly.

"What gives?" I asked queasily. I harbored great hopes that everything was over, but suspected otherwise.

Grant scowled. "Ragnarok's been blocked. I should have known. I really should have known."

"Oh."

It wasn't over.

We hit pavement with a bump, and the environment began to look civilized, even domestic. We drove past a sumptuous contemporary house set up on a ridge. Farther on, more houses appeared.

I saw a street sign: MULHOLLAND DR.

Jill asked, "Grant, any idea where we should be heading? I think we're going east."

"I'm famished," I said when Grant didn't answer.

"Me, too," Jill agreed. "Grant?"

"Huh? Oh, yeah. You guys go ahead and eat. I've got to fix this up right now."

"Okay. I'm going to head back down into the valley. There's this terrific rib place in Van Nuys. Jeez, what time is it?"

The car's digital clock showed 11:29 A.M., and my watch wouldn't have been more than two minutes off had I been mindful to set it back to Pacific Time.

"You want lunch?" Jill asked me.

"I want lunch."

"Then we'll have lunch."

She made the next left, which I saw was Beverly Glen Canyon Road. I began to recognize it as the road we had taken up from Ventura Boulevard last night. Serpentine and steep, it coiled down the dizzying slopes of Sherman Oaks.

"You'll love these ribs. Authentic Texas barbecue."

"Will I dream of Lyndon Johnson?"

Jill laughed. "Let's hope not. Why did you say that?"

"Oh, you know, I thought it might be like eating Welsh rarebit."

"Oh."

"Goddamn it."

I glanced back at Grant, who had uttered the god-damn it, and did a take. He seemed a bit insubstantial. Again, I rubbed my eyes, just like cartoon characters do, and looked again. He was fuzzy, blurred, fading in and out of existence. Yet he still held the computer in his hands. It didn't seem to fade in and out so much, though I could have been mistaken.

"Grant?"

"Huh? No, it's nothing. Just having a devil of a time making things work. Merlin has been busy, and very clever as usual."

"Grant, tell me something."

Without looking up Grant answered, "Yeah, go ahead."

"That stuff we went through back there, the monster, the alien planet—it was real, wasn't it?"

"Uh . . . well, yeah. Kind of."

"Kind of. How real is 'kind of'?"

"As real as anything gets. We're going to have to redefine reality when we get done with this."

"Grant, I hate to tell you this, but you're fading away."

"I'll be fluctuating for some time to come. Don't let it worry you. I'll still be with you in spirit, as the say-ing goes."

"You still need us, don't you? We can't go home."

"I kind of wish you'd stick around for a bit longer, true."

u "Grant, I don't want to stick around."

"Yeah, I know. No way I can hold you here."

"You can haunt me."

"True enough. But I wouldn't haunt my friends with-out just cause."

I turned forward again and exuded a painful sigh. The

day was young but fatigue had settled in my bones; also, I had a colossal thirst. Scouting for convenience stores, I saw none until we got down into the flats, where Jill told me that the restaurant she had in mind was not far away. Could I wait? I could wait, but not much longer. My mouth was setting up a diorama of the Mojave.

Meanwhile it was good to be back in the real world, and this reality had a gritty megalopolitan edge to it. Endless storefronts, businesses, strip malls, mile after mile of contemporary urban sprawl. No hills, no prominent elevations that I could see. I got the impression that LA was absolutely flat where it was not intimidatingly mountainous. Again, this was a first-time visitor's impression.

We passed numerous convenience stores, wherein coolers full of Pepsi and Mountain Dew and Nehi Grape and Canada Dry ginger ale and Coke and Gatorade and Dole fruit juice, all glistening with frost in their convenient aluminum cans or recyclable glass containers, sang songs that Odysseus never heard. I wanted to chain myself to the seat and seal Jill's ears with wax. My mouth was parched. Another convenience store rolled by, then another. COLD BEER, a sign murmured to me.

"Are we there yet?" I wanted to know.

This brought a crooked smile to Jill's face. Making her laugh was easy but enjoyable. I felt childlike, a little mischievous. I wanted to have some fun. What I most emphatically did not want was a reprise of the crazed "reality" we had just escaped. Here I was in Los Angeles, one of the biggest cities in the world, a city like no other; a city of dreams, but all those were made of celluloid acetate and had the pleasant habit of *staying* celluloid acetate, for the most part. I wanted to do normal LA things: go to Disneyland, do Knott's Berry Farm, take the Universal Tour, get shot at on the freeway by a drive-by gunman. I could handle all that. I most emphatically did not want to lose my mind and possibly die at the hands of some galumphing horror turned real by cheapjack magic tricks run through a video game.

What was I saying? That couldn't happen. Things like that don't happen in the real world. They simply don't.

Finally, the rib place, which had an overlong and absurd name and whose physical plant was unprepossessing, to say the least. The parking lot was full, though, which I took as a good sign. A restaurant with an empty parking lot advertises its bad food. Jill parked across the street.

"Grant, are you coming in?"

"Uh, no, Jill. I've found that I've had very little appetite since I died."

I reached out and grabbed his arm—a trifle roughly, I'm afraid.

"You seem corporeal enough to me."

"You're in the Net now, dude. Okay, see that homeless person over there?"

"Huh? Oh. I see him. Why?"

"Call him over."

"Uh . . ."

"Go ahead."

I did. It was a man of, say, thirty-five, with facial lines that made him look fifty. Otherwise nondescript, save that his clothes were rumpled and underlaundered. He came over readily enough, though with an air of cautious skepticism.

"Yes, sir?"

"This gentleman in the backseat would like a word with you."

The guy glanced behind me, looked at me, then turned away.

"Yeah," the homeless man said. "Yeah, listen . . ."

I looked back. Grant was grinning smugly at me.

"Okay, here." I reached in my pocket and found some change. "There you go, pal."

The man took the change. "Hey, thank you, good buddy. Thanks a lot." He walked away.

Jill said, "Grant, did he see you or not? I couldn't tell."

Grant shrugged. "I don't think he wanted to see me."

"Grant," I said, "what does it take to get a straight answer out of you?"

"Ask me the right questions."

"God, I'm thirsty," Jill said.

"Can't imagine why," I said. "Let's go."

We crossed the wide boulevard, went into the restaurant, and chose a booth along the front window. The place was medium-crowded. It smelled like a good restaurant. You can tell a good place by the smell.

The first thing we ordered was water, which we drank with much onomatopoeia, then ordered more.

Jill made a face. "I don't believe I'm drinking LA tap water."

"It's wet," I said. "What's good on the menu?"

"Everything. The beef ribs, especially. And the sausage."

"I'll have both."

We ordered both, with fries and coleslaw. The waitress, a quondam perky blond, well past her prime perk, had what I took to be a Texas accent. No, born in Albuquerque, raised in Phoenix. Well, close, I decided in my geographically myopic mind.

We didn't talk much while waiting, content to stare

out the window and languidly sip our delicious tap water, which no doubt was chock full of minerals good for growing young wizards. Traffic passed, as did a few more "homeless" people. Well, I didn't know that they weren't for a fact. They did have a rootless look about them.

The food came fairly quickly, and was good. Very good. This was Texas-style barbecue? I suddenly had new sympathy and admiration for Lyndon Baines Johnson, who, as I remembered, regularly threw vast saturnalias on his ranch featuring this fine cuisine. One does not ordinarily get beef ribs. The barbecue sauce was excellent, and the sausage, to use a regionalism, was *special*.

I ate happily. I didn't know what was going on in the various universes—

What about that notion, to the effect that there may be more than one universe? Linguistically suspect. Because the word "universe" itself . . .

Forget it, I told myself. All right, wherever the main show was going on, this universe or another, I didn't know what was going on there, and did not care at the moment.

For the next few minutes I thought of nothing but the food until there was no more food to think about, or eat. I sat back, belched unabashedly, and sipped the rest of my Coke.

Sotto voce, Jill said, "You should see this guy." With a slight tilt of her head, she indicated the booth behind me.

I took my time about turning around to look, but finally did, as casually and as unobviously as I could. My jaw dropped.

"Hi, there!"

It was the strange man. The blue of his eyes seemed to have lightened a shade, or several. They were now a pale watery blue. I don't ordinarily notice people's eye coloring but had somehow recently picked up the habit. There was something about this guy's eyes that disturbed me. Also Grant's, now that I thought of it.

His suit this time was saffron yellow, and the hat was a white skimmer. He wore a turquoise four-in-hand with embroidered silver lamé diamonds. The carnation was white now, whiter than his hair, which in this light appeared yellowish white.

"Oh, God."

He laughed. "Couldn't be the food. Had a bad day so far? It might get better. On the other hand—"

"It just got worse."

"Actually, it's been rather boring so far. At least I'm of that opinion. Dueling computer programmers. Not exactly the stuff of epics."

"It's been more than epic," I said. "It's been Homeric. By the way, I've decided you're not Jones."

"I told you I wasn't."

"Who are you?"

"As I also said before, an interested observer."

"What's your stake?"

"A world. A world that was once lost and now can be regained."

"Who lost it?"

"Principalities, powers." He grinned. "You'll learn in time."

"Are you God or the devil? Better yet, do you run a government regulatory agency?"

He chuckled. "You have a wit, sir. A fine wit."

I turned around. "I don't know whether I'm glad that you see him," I said to Jill.

"This is the guy who gave you trouble?"

"None other."

"Hello," Jill called to him, smiling pleasantly.

"Hello to you. Fine day."

"Yes. Do you have a name?"

"Call me Arman."

"Arman, what do you want from us?"

I turned to look at him.

Arman settled back in his booth and lifted his water glass. He peered into it. "At this point I'm merely observing. Don't pay me any special mind."

"Hard to avoid," I said, "when you keep making a pest of yourself."

His face hardened a bit. It was still an improbable face. He put me in mind of Oscar Wilde as played by a cross between Laurence Olivier and Cyril Ritchard.

"I don't like your rudeness," he said.

"Oh, excuse me."

"Irony noted. We may be adversaries but we can be civil."

"Listen," I said. "If you're not Lloyd Merlin Jones, do you know him?"

He took a delicate sip of water—the ice of which seemed to sparkle in the glass, faintly. "Yes, I know Merlin. He works for me. Or I for him." He cast aside a short chuckle. "Sometimes I'm not sure of the relationship."

"Did he conjure you?"

"Oh . . ." Arman thought about it as he viewed a pleasant prospect of the street life of Van Nuys, California, one of our finest American cities. "I suppose you could say that."

"So, you're . . . what, a demon?"

This produced from him a painful snigger. His manner was as though I had uttered something wildly outrageous.

"Have I misspoken?" I asked.

I waited for an answer but none seemed forthcoming, so I tried another tack.

"Are you real or are you a figment of my imagination and Jill's?"

This he only sneered at.

"All right, let's put it this way," I doggedly persisted. "Are you . . . what's the phrase?—software wildfowl?"

"Wild*life*," he corrected with a dyspeptic and disapproving frown. "Do you believe in Sherlock Holmes?"

"What?"

Arman was patient. "I said, do you believe in Sherlock Holmes?"

"What exactly do you mean?"

"Do you believe he existed?"

"No."

"Who didn't exist?"

"Huh? Sherlock Holmes didn't exist. He was a fictional character."

" '*He* was a fictional character.' Now, what I'd like you to do is this. Examine that sentence. Analyze it, parse it. When you perceive the paradox you will, paradoxically, understand me and my kind. I'm afraid that's all I'm going to say about that for now. Is the food here good?"

"Try the beef ribs," I told him.

"I will. Have a nice day."

I turned around, scanned the place for our waitress, but didn't see her.

"What now?" I said, not expecting anything but a shrug in answer, which Jill dutifully gave me.

"Obviously we have to talk to Grant," she said.

I looked across the street at our car. I couldn't see Grant from this angle.

"Right. You know, he doesn't—" I stopped, noticing

Jill's expression, then turned to see what she was gawking at.

Coming toward us was our waitress, or at least part of her. The body was the same but the blond hair and the sad-tired but still pretty face was gone, replaced by the head of some animal. An auroch, I thought. Something ancient, almost mythical.

"Anything else I can get you?"

The voice was the same, the animal mouth moved in perfect sync with the human voice, forming each phoneme. I shook my head.

"Okay, thank you very much, sir."

I looked down at the check that had been placed in front of me.

"Sir, is something wrong?"

I looked up at the ghastly thing.

"Uh, no, nothing. Thank you. Here, keep the change."

"Thanks! You come back, now. Bye!"

We got up and began walking out. This time Arman did not pull his disappearing act. As we passed he was tucking into a plate of ribs and sausage. I had not seen him being served.

He grinned at us. "These *are* special."

16

ONCE OUTSIDE WE LOOKED UP TO SEE PUFFY LACTIF-erous clouds swirling through the sky; they looked like dollops of cream in coffee. Above them, the sky was a distinct shade of green.

"Unusual for LA," Jill said.

"Looks like a twister brewing," I commented.

"You're joking. In LA?"

Pinkish clouds began to intermix, and the sky took on an ominous tone. The urban landscape seemed strange as well. Everything had the look of a high-contrast photograph. Grays evaporated, whereas above there was every shade of gray marbled in among the pinks and the greens.

Jill observed all this and finally pronounced: "This isn't LA." She opened the unlocked door and got into the car.

I got in, too, and only then realized that Grant was gone. Jill and I exchanged bemused looks and scanned our respective vistas of the street. No amiable specters in sight.

"Grant?" Jill said tentatively.

No answer came. The laptop lay on the backseat and I picked it up. The screen was alive with multicolored cryptic symbols, swarming in patterns. I had not noticed the color capability before. As far as I knew, the laptop's screen was monochromatic. The plastic case felt tingly, and it glowed with a faint greenish light, as though it bore traces of radium; or perhaps the strange light from the sky produced this effect.

As I watched, the parade of symbols and glyphs regrouped to form into a word.

DRIVE

I showed it to Jill. She nodded and started the car.

I studied the screen. "Drive, he said. But in what direction?"

"There's only one direction," Jill answered. "Toward Jones's place."

"Did you say you didn't know exactly where it is?"

"I have the street address. It's Laurelwood Drive, which has got to be somewhere off Laurel Canyon, or thereabouts. The thing that's confusing is that Merlin drops mention of his place now and then, and he always talks about the great view he has, how nice the place is. I've looked on the map and it doesn't look like Laurelwood has a view, unless I looked wrong and it threads up into the heights. Or it could be a different Laurelwood."

"Maps aren't always unambiguous or entirely accurate. And street patterns can be confusing. But do you think you can find it?"

"Yeah, sure, with a little searching."

I tilted my head back against the padded headrest and contemplated the velvet-swathed underside of the roof. A great weary exhalation left me.

"I suppose we're committed to this," I said.

Jill went through a moment's rumination before saying, "I guess I am. I guess I care about the Net, and think it's important."

"What are the stakes, Jill? Why is this important?"

"A whole new universe is opening up. I think this is real. I believe in it."

"I think you do," I said. "But I have my doubts. Not sure I want to believe in it."

"After what you've seen?"

I looked at her. "Have you ever heard of *folie à deux?*"

"Shared delusion. That's what you think this is?"

"I hope it is, because I don't want to live with the ramifications of its being real."

"It's real, Skye. I've been in the Net for two years, and it isn't delusion. I've done things, talked with unseen beings, foreseen future events. I've even . . ." One corner of her mouth turned up.

"What?" I prompted.

"Once I cast a love charm. There was this woman I wanted to meet. To make love to, really. She was beautiful and I fell madly in love with her. Met her at a faculty party. But she—"

"Jill, you have to start thinking of group delusion."

"You don't believe me?"

"Jill, it's not a question of my believing you."

"Skye, listen to this. I wanted that woman. At the party we didn't hit it off at all. I guess I was nervous. She seemed to dislike me. But I went home and worked a spell on my computer. She called within minutes, Skye. Minutes. I hadn't given her my number."

I sighed. "All very well and good, but that proves nothing, means nothing."

"You've been talking to Grant, you *saw* Grant, for God's sake. How is that possible if this is all a hallucination?"

"I knew Grant well, and I'm perfectly capable of recreating him. So are you."

"But something killed Grant."

"A bear. A serial killer. The mob."

"You don't believe that, Skye. I know you don't."

I looked out at the cityscape as it became transfigured, growing ever stranger and more unreal. It now took on the bold colors and primitive immediacy of certain paintings by *les Fauves*. We passed a Matisse burger joint, a Braque car dealership, then a big furniture store that shaded into the Impressionists. Iridescent reds and purples massed, pulsated, their disparate wavelengths distressing my retinas.

Ah. This, then, was "tripping." I had always wondered about drug experiences, never having indulged in hallucinogens when it was fashionable the first time. (The fad seems to have made a comeback of late.) Vibrant colors, colors bleeding from one to the other, a general soft edge to things, a graininess, a general fuzziness. This was the experience without the chemical and with none of the risks. None of the usual risks, anyway.

"This is great," Jill said, and this time I was ambivalent about hearing her second what I was seeing. I was not at all sure I wanted to share these or any experiences with her.

Truth to tell, though, I was rather enjoying the show; for the moment.

Styles shifted. A Mondrian office building . . . a Monet car wash—the palette was always light, very light. Some Cubist tendencies began to turn up. Nowhere was there Dutch Masters dreariness; no Rembrandt, no chiaroscuro etchings by candlelight, no earthy dirt colors, no burnt umber, no proletarian early van Gogh; but lots and lots of daubs and dots and pastel pointillism.

We toured a Lautrecian arrondissement, traversing its wide boulevards, and along one of these we passed a roseate structure that resembled an old mill: a resurrected Moulin Rouge? Meanwhile, above all this, cyclonic inversions massed and piled, clouds shot through with yellow and orange set amongst patches of exotic shades of green, the whole mess streaked with gray through which veins of silver branched.

Jill made a left on what I thought to be Ventura Boulevard. It never looked so colorful. I saw a storefront on the far side of the street with a sign over it that read—unless I was badly mistaken—FEARFUL APPARITIONS. Exactly. There was an underlying suggestion of danger in all this.

The screen was doing other interesting things now: moiré patterns alternating with chevron formations. I wondered what it all meant, if it meant anything at all.

"Something following us," Jill said, looking at the rearview mirror.

I looked back and noted that a vehicle of sorts was pacing us. The thing was a marriage of tank and circus wagon, if that makes any sense, garishly done up in polka dots and multicolored stripes.

"I don't know what that is," Jill said, "but I don't like it."

Her right boot came down heavy on the accelerator. We raced down the boulevard. I watched more colorful architecture go by; even the seedy-looking places were brilliantly painted, and it occurred to me that the country could win at least half the battle against inner-city decay by spending a few million per city on paint. It might cheer everyone up, stimulate thinking along more positive lines. As the more liberal-minded of our countrymen like to say, it could be done for the price of one supersonic nuclear bomber.

Jill turned right hard, making the tires screech. I grabbed the handhold above the door. Handy thing. I hung on as she roared around another corner.

I looked back. The strange vehicle was keeping up with us. It handled corners very well, using its many oversize wheels and strips of metal tread to best advantage.

"I'll try to make the freeway," Jill said. "That thing looks too big to fit on the ramp."

"Uh, don't be too sure," I said.

I looked back again and was puzzled to see that the thing had sprouted a flashing red light atop its turret. A siren began to wail.

"What the hell is this?" Jill wanted to know.

"You'd better pull over. It could be the cops."

"Since when do cops drive squad cars like that?"

"In this dream sequence, they might. In the real world, it's probably a black-and-white."

Jill shook her head. "That thing's not real."

She floored the accelerator and we raced along a residential street that looked like an illustration out of a children's book: split levels with crayon-colored siding, garages for toy cars, crepe paper lawns. A sign flashed past: SPEED LIMIT 15.

"If it's not real, Jill, why are we running from it?"

The siren continued to whoop as Jill made a series of turns. I hung on, my right shoulder banging against the door, left thigh whacking against the gearshift when Jill wheeled the other way. The tires chirped and chittered. White smoke began to trail out the back of the car. I glanced at the speedometer. She was hitting 70 mph on the straightaways.

I noticed that traffic was light. Just a few cars, which Jill easily whipped around. No, this couldn't be Los Angeles. At this time of day traffic should be as thick as ants swarming around a disturbed anthill.

The bizarre vehicle behind us kept up the chase, defying disbelief that something so bulky could move so fast. But apparently this was not your garden-variety circus calliope-wagon/self-propelled howitzer-cum–patrol car; which, by the way, now sported paisley fenders, raked airfoils along the side, a sequined gun turret, and huge twin chromium exhaust pipes that gleamed in the sun. A few seconds later I looked back again to find that the vehicle had acquired even more doodads; it was now set about with vents, periscopes, antennae, plastic bubbles, and not a few neon-colored propellers. It could have been an entry in a surreal event that combined the Rose Parade and the now-defunct October Revolution *tour de force* through Red Square. (Come to think of it, we weren't all that far from Pasadena.)

Jill made another quick turn, this time onto a street under construction. She swerved around a sawhorse barrier but ran over a mound of rubble. The right side of the car reared up and slammed down, altering our vector. We headed toward the curb and a rendezvous with several parked cars. At the last second Jill straightened out and kept going.

"Jill, Jesus Christ!"

"Sorry."

We roared through another Day-Glo Montmartre, then hung a left and alarmed the deracinated intelligentsia having aperitifs in the cafes along a street in Montparnasse—they weren't visible buy my mind sketched them in. No, this wasn't Paris but whoever was controlling the color scheme definitely had a thing for the late nineteenth century French palette.

"Jill, it's gaining. You've got to pull over."

"Don't be a weenie."

"I'm going to be a *dead* weenie in one second."

It was a prophetic statement. Something big pulled out onto the street ahead of us—a neon-orange garbage truck. Jill swerved, skidded, and went out of control. The car did a 180-degree turnabout, then rolled backward until it slammed against a garbage dumpster and stopped.

I bounced and slid, ending up on the floor, my seat belt having snapped open.

"Goddamn it, Jill, take it easy!"

"You want whatever's in there to get us?"

"I don't want to be squashed inside a Toyota!"

"I should have got the midsize," she said ruefully.

Jill gunned the engine as I tried to get up. She banged the automatic transmission into drive and I almost flipped over into the backseat. I hit my crown against the roof, and, as the car turned, Newton's laws plastered me against the door.

I yelled, "You insane bitch!" (Insert this and other epithets at random into the next sequence.) I was quite beside myself.

We flashed along another spacious thoroughfare, swerving for a truck or two, then bore left when the way diverged.

I chanced a look back. The contraption that pursued us had transcended surrealism and was now edging into the realm of the alarmingly peculiar. I did not want to look at it any more.

I glanced at Jill. She was moving her lips, muttering something over and over. It sounded like a chant. Her mantra?

I saw a sign: FREEWAY ENTRANCE. A second later Jill careened right and sent us hurtling up a ramp. There was a red light at the juncture with the highway but that was as nothing to speed demon Jill. She tramped the accelerator and we barged into a stream of traffic that looked more normal for the time and the location, yet still a bit on the thin side. Perhaps LA has its good traffic days? At any rate, such was my conjecture.

Reluctantly, I cast a glance backward. The goofy gizmo had made it up the two-lane–wide ramp easily enough; but perhaps Jill had other ideas, such as getting off the freeway via a more narrow ramp?—but again this was conjecture on my part. If that demented contraption back there was, in reality, an L.A.P.D. black-and-white, they had us. They'd set up roadblocks at all the exits, dispatch motorcycle police, and so on. Surely Jill had watched prime-time TV during the last few decades. I mean, who among us isn't familiar with the many and varied practices and procedures of the Los Angeles Police Department, or the California Highway Patrol, or any of the various law enforcement agencies and judicial systems in and about, or having jurisdiction in and for the city and county of Los Angeles, California? Not very goddamned many people, that's who.

Except crazy Jill, who thought she could beat the system.

We zoomed down the freeway—which freeway, I knew not. The San Diego, the Santa Monica, the Ventura? I didn't know the city, hadn't a clue where in the hell we were. All about me was a megaurban panorama: miles and miles and miles of concrete road; involuted, spaghetti-like interchanges; six lanes of traffic rushing pell-mell to nowhere at 70 mph, bumper-to-bumper; or stalled, going nowhere, bumper-to-bumper. That is how the LA freeway system now presented itself to me, in one transmogrified, polychrome, telescoped experience. I seemed to be perceiving the entire system at once. I saw flying ramps, borne on precarious stanchions, soaring through the air, intertwining, curving, feeding the circulation to other roadways and bringing fresh blood to ours. I saw lanes diverge and meld and diverge again; awestruck, I watched highways by the dozen flow over my head and under my feet. It was a maze, it was a farrago. It was a mess.

The pink polka-dot tank still dogged our every evasion, expertly weaving through traffic. Another red whirling light flashed behind it.

"They have backup," I told Jill.

"Still not real," she said, her teeth clenched. For some reason I now noticed that she had a thin mouth, lips pale and thin. She seemed grimly determined to see this through.

I thought she was completely psychotic.

I cast about desperately in my mind for ways to escape, to get free of this madness. I had missed my chance when we had spun out. That would have been a good time to jump ship. I would only have broken an arm or a leg. Too late now. Jumping out would get me killed.

The cops—as I now believed our pursuers to be—were gaining. I would be probably be killed anyway, smashed against an abutment, dead in a paradigm high-speed chase, for which this city was notorious.

Jill began her mantra again. Or was it an incantation? Her lips barely moved, forming syllables I could not make out.

The landscape continued to change. All I saw now was freeway, spreading out to the mountains. In every direction I turned I saw high-speed, limited-access highways and their various whorls and arabesques. Some looked like roller coasters, dipping and climbing. I looked ahead and saw a roadway curve up and back on itself, doing a 360-degree loop like some latter-day thrill ride. As we neared this anomaly I gradually understood, to my rising horror, that our roadway led to it.

"You can't be serious about . . . *that*," I said.

"What? Oh. Don't worry, Skye, what you're seeing doesn't necessary correspond to reality, one-to-one. You have to keep that in mind."

What I had in mind was the galaxy of flashing red lights that now swarmed after us, the entire highway patrol out in force on an all-points bulletin. I did not bother trying to discern what else besides the fairy tank was back there. I was only mildly interested in knowing. I could wait.

I looked forward. We were heading into the loop. As the roadway rose dramatically in front of us, I frantically tried to lock my seat belt. I succeeded just in time.

I don't know what happened because I shut my eyes. I felt an unnatural tug upward, then down again. When I opened my eyes again the loop was behind us. I didn't want to ask Jill what had happened.

"See? That wasn't so bad." Jill was grinning at me. She looked positively deranged.

We drove and drove. I saw a sign: HOLLYWOOD FREEWAY. Jill veered and our direction changed.

We drove and drove. The ride seemed endless now. I would ride forever, in thrall to this female Jehu and her magic chariot.

Another sign: HARBOR FREEWAY. We drove and drove. Another eternity passed. I was in agony, pure agony.

I checked the rear. The red flashing lights were falling back. I breathed again. A signpost dead ahead.

SANTA MONICA FREEWAY

"Where are we going?" I asked.
"Santa Monica," she said.

17

*T*HINGS BEGAN TO LOOK NORMAL AGAIN. THE PSYCH-
edelic colors faded and vegetable browns and greens
reasserted themselves. The distant mountains turned
gray-green and brown. Gray smog appeared, a soft floating blanket of haze covering everything.

We passed a stand of palm trees. The faint smell of
the sea came to my nostrils. Salt, dead fishy things.

We got off the freeway and slowed. This place seemed
even sunnier than the Valley or LA. Buildings were
white, streets were wide, swept with sea breezes. The
urban forest still looked overgrown here, high rises all
the way up to the beach, but you could tell that this was
an old seaside town. Jill made a series of turns, driving
now at a sane and normal speed. She found an almost
empty parking lot by the beach and pulled in.

I looked out at the sea. It was blue and beautiful, and
I felt as though some new planet had swum into my ken.
An inveterate landlubber, this was my first time laying
eyes on the Pacific.

Jill parked, turned off the ignition. We both wilted.

"I don't believe we're still alive," I said, my eyes
closed.

"Had my mojo working."

"Eh?"

of her well-rounded buttocks, worth more than a few glimpses. I felt a very distant, wistful pang of arousal, which faded quickly.

I gave her time to get into her jeans, looking back when I heard the zip of a zipper.

The soaked shorts went into her carry-on. She dropped to her knees and sat primping her hair, looking out to sea.

"I love the ocean," she said. "God, I wish I lived here."

"Here, in Santa Monica?"

"No. Up the coast. Santa Barbara's nice. Or down the coast. Trouble is, too damned many people have the same idea."

"California is a dream. It's never a reality."

"When I get my doctorate I'm going to try mightily to get up to Oregon. Eugene is wonderful."

I was on my back, letting the sky fill my field of vision. There was nothing in that sky. Nothing. "Never met the fellow."

"Huh? Very droll. Do you like it here?"

I grunted.

"Not for everybody, I guess." She was silent for a few moments, then said, "I'm thirsty."

I was, too, but I asked, "What language was that you were chanting in?"

"Hebrew."

"I assumed you weren't Jewish."

"I'm not, but I like the cabala. Jewish magic. It's my favorite magical system."

"Oh, magic comes in systems?"

"Sure. Everything comes in systems."

"Don't they tend to be mutually incompatible?"

"To some extent, just like computer systems. But

I think different ways of doing magic are just that—different ways of doing the same thing."

"Where did you get this magic? How'd you find out about it?"

"From a book called the *Sefer Hazohar*. I had it scanned into files for my computer, then I worked with it."

"You didn't get the book from MagicNet?"

"No. The cabala's really not secret anymore. Well, maybe parts of it are. There are still practitioners in the Near East, old rabbis and such. They might be guarding secret stuff. But you can research anything. Have you ever heard of it?

"I've heard of it but never looked into it. Does Merlin do cabala?"

"No. That's one of the reasons I use it."

"You said his big crotchet was Persian magic?"

"Yeah, he's really into esoteric stuff. Zoroastrianism."

I scooped up some sand. "Another subject I don't know much about, and what I've read is mostly forgotten."

"I don't know much either. I know he spent time in Iran on an archaeological dig, before that country got to be a dangerous place for Westerners. Must have been in his undergraduate days."

I let the sand run through my fingers. "Then the magic that Merlin works is Zoroastrian?"

Jill thought about it. "I think he's combined some systems. Grant would know, since Grant works in the same system."

" 'Ragnarok' isn't a name from Persian mythology. Scandinavian."

"As I said, you can combine mythologies."

I brushed sand from my hands, opened the carry-ing bag, and took out the laptop. The screen had got curiouser. Pictograms, even pictures. A winged, lionlike animal walked in animation across the screen. A griffin? Yes, a griffin.

Jill looked at it and nodded. "Looks Persian."

"Grant, are you there? Can you hear me?"

Slowly, the screen formed these words, composed of various and disparate glyphs and icons:

DANGER NOW

I said, "Well, that's an answer, I think."

"Yes, definitely."

I looked out to sea. A few whitecaps farther out. The sun was declining, throwing webs of silvery reflection across the water.

"Jill?"

"Yes?"

"Teach me to do magic."

"Well, it takes a while to learn. What is it you want to do?"

"I feel vulnerable. I want protection."

She nodded. "What's protection to you? What would make you feel safe and secure?"

"Nothing. But I want something, a weapon."

"Do you really think that a gun will do anything?"

I looked at her. "How did you know I was talking about a gun? Though you're right, I was. But not just any gun. A magic gun."

"Oh. Then conjure one. This is the Net. Anything can happen, if you want it to. If a gun is a symbol of security for you, then maybe you need one."

"It's never been a symbol of security for me. I'm not a gun fancier, never was. But I fancy one now."

"Then create one. You have the power."

The only gun I could think of at the moment was Ellison's curious piece.

Jill said, "I've heard of magic swords, daggers, that kind of thing, but I don't exactly know what a magic gun would be like."

One that shoots silver bullets, of course."

She gave a big nod of understanding, then suddenly giggled. "Didn't the guy with the mask, what was his name—?"

"Of course, but he was a mythic figure himself, wasn't he?"

She smiled, nodding again.

"Right," I said. "Now all I have to do is conjure my magic gun, which shoots magic bullets. Step One . . ."

"Just believe," Jill told me.

"Just believe," I repeated. "Okay. I guess I believe."

"No guessing. You either believe or you don't."

"Right. Is there an incantation?"

"Not if you don't want one. I've found magic to be mostly mental. It's all in the mind."

"It's all in the mind," I droned.

"You're being silly."

"I'm not being silly. It's all in the mind."

The problem was that my mind had always been of a hard, skeptical-rationalist temper, regarding magic, astrology, and even ESP phenomena as essentially bogus. They were hoaxes, delusions, evidence of the congenital madness of crowds. I would not even say that I kept an "open mind" about such things. I had looked into various flaps over the years, from spiritualism to UFOs, and found them all to be wanting of empirical proof. In time, I had simply closed those mental files with no intention of ever opening them again in the absence of startlingly new data (and the data in these areas are *never* new).

Now, however, startling events confronted me, demanding an explanation; and I had no explanation, except this: that Jill was a magician, and so were her friends and enemies, and all of this was quite real.

In short, I now believed.

There was no hocus-pocus, no puff of smoke, no sparkle of fairy dust. Ellison's strange gun simply materialized in my hands. I had not realized that I was holding them out to receive it.

"Wow," Jill said quietly.

I looked the thing over. The stock was brown plastic, the barrel of blued steel. The bolt was easy to draw back, which I did. There was one round in the chamber, and I took it out. The cartridge was identical to the one Ellison had showed us, save that the projectile was silver.

"Unbelievable," Jill said.

"I'm a conjurer," I said.

"You are. You must have some kind of talent to pull that off, first time."

"You're a good teacher. Well, now I have my weapon. What shall I do with it?"

Jill turned her head toward the ocean. "Fog," she said.

I looked. A rolling bank of mist was making its way toward shore, moving fast, too fast to be a natural phenomenon.

"Something's up," she said.

"We'd better get moving."

She agreed. She carried her boots and jacket and I hauled both bags, having put the gun in with the computer and its peripherals. We ran.

By the time we reached the car the fog had enshrouded the beach. After we had piled in and just as Jill started the engine, the fog overtook us and we could see nothing beyond the hood. All around was total white-out.

"Shit." Jill slid the car into gear, but hesitated. There was no question of driving in soup as thick as this.

"I have a feeling this stuff is not going to lift anytime soon," I said.

"I have a feeling you're right. We have to do something."

"For instance?"

"Not taking anything away from your budding talent, I think the climate is changing. The magical climate. It's going to be a free-for-all."

"Oh?"

I didn't quite like the sound of that.

"But that gives us some advantages," she added.

Jill twisted a switch on the turn signal lever and the dashboard lights came on, as did the headlights. She began to chant again.

At first the headlights merely reflected back, and the fog was as impenetrable as before; but within half a minute the mists began to recede, and very soon a circular area with a radius of about thirty feet around the car had cleared away.

"Enough visibility to drive by," Jill said confidently.

It looked like just enough, if she took it easy. She didn't of course. She whipped the car out of the lot and into the street.

"What I think we have to do," she said as she wove through deserted city streets, "is get above the fog. Up into the hills. We'll go up the Coast Highway and take one of the canyon roads back to the Valley."

"You're the driver."

"Trust me," she said.

I did, now, more or less; but I asked myself whether

conjured fogs (and this had to be one) hugged the shore as did mundane ones. Or can they invade the heights, and do generally what they damn well please? I was persuaded as to the latter possibility.

18

SOMEHOW WE GOT DOWN TO THE SHORE AGAIN and headed north, leaving Santa Monica behind, and with it the fog, which dissipated as abruptly as it had come. I got the notion that there is a limit to the rate at which magical weather phenomena can advance along a front; either that or the reigning weather demiurge hadn't anticipated our moving out so quickly.

High sheer cliffs, eroded and unstable, loomed over the Coast Highway. Houses bravely stood near the edge. I was astonished to see the end of one concrete patio jutting out into space, the cliff crumbling away beneath it. Makeshift stanchions held it up now, a desperate effort by the owner to stave off disaster. One day, though, he would have the same worry about his house.

The Pacific to our left, we arched northwest along the curve of the shore, toward mythical Malibu and its surfing mystery cult. Lined along the highway, beach houses blocked our view of the surf. Traffic thinned out as we drove.

"Aren't we a long way from Studio City, or wherever we're going?"

Jill answered, "Yeah, but Topanga Canyon Road will take us all the way back to Ventura Boulevard."

"Oh."

"We just make—Oh, damn."

Another fog bank rolled in from the sea, and we could not veer away. There was no way of turning east. This goop was positively viscous. It clung to the car, frosting the windshield. Jill's magic succeeded in fending it off, but it kept pushing back tenaciously.

"We'll never make it to Topanga," she said.

I opened the glove compartment and rummaged through the rental agency paperwork until it yielded a complimentary city map.

"Find out if there's a turnoff before Topanga," she said.

"Will try."

The map was difficult to read until my sense of orientation firmed up. I found Santa Monica and ran my finger north.

"Does Los Flores Canyon Road sound familiar?" I asked.

"Never been up there. Is it before Topanga?"

"Sure looks like it."

"Great. Hey, is that it?"

"Looks like a parking lot."

She drove for another quarter mile before saying, "Here it comes, maybe."

The next turnoff did look promising. Jill slowed and wheeled right. There was something at the corner that looked like a road sign, but I couldn't make out the lettering.

"Is this Los Flores?"

I shook my head. "Don't know."

"Well, it's got to get us up and away from this."

It got us up, and the fog began to thin out. The road commenced a steep, wiggly climb.

Suddenly, something hit me. "Oh, my God."

Jill turned her head, one dark eyebrow arched, then looked back at the road. "What is it?"

I said nothing as I massaged my forehead.

"Skye? Are you all right?"

"Yeah. Something just hit me. I didn't call Sharon. Didn't even think of her."

"Girlfriend?"

I nodded. "I have not given Sharon one thought since I last saw her yesterday. Not one single, solitary thought."

"Don't worry about it. Let's face it, a lot of crap has hit the fan."

"I can't understand how I could do that. Forget like that."

"Are you very close? You don't live with her, do you?"

"No. No, she has her own place. It's just—I can't fucking understand it. It's as if she didn't exist."

"Will she be worried?"

"She'll certainly wonder what the hell happened to me."

"You should phone. But I guess this isn't the best place to look for a phone."

We had reached heights that the fog had not. The road coiled far above and I could begin to make out the extent of the mountain range we were climbing. There were trees up here, and some were of good size. They looked like oaks.

"Pretty," I said.

"It's nice up in this area."

I gave a look back. I saw nothing but the fog that chased us but which lost ground with every passing moment.

I looked ahead again and something seemed to have

happened. The sides of the canyon looked craggy and wild and the trees were gone.

"What happened?"

"I don't know," Jill said. "I saw it change this time. It was sudden."

"Are we heading for Vasquez again?"

"Maybe, but this looks more like Utah or Arizona than California."

I had to agree—for the time being, anyway; because over the next few minutes the landscape underwent a gradual sea change. The coloration of the rocks turned a few shades darker, losing pinks and tans and picking up grays and browns. The sky darkened as well. Watching produced a strange feeling, as of looking over the shoulder of an omnipotent creator in the act of creation.

"Uh-oh."

I looked at Jill, who was eyeing the dashboard with alarm. "What's up?"

"Water temperature. It's almost into the red."

"Overheating?"

"Yes, unless this gauge has gone bad."

"Somehow I doubt that."

We continued to climb; I kept my eye on the gauge. The motor continued to work normally, but when the temperature needle edged into the warning zone I looked up and saw a wisp of white smoke trail from the front of the hood.

"We're definitely overheating," I said. "The odometer reads low mileage. This is practically a new car. Must have been an assembly-line goof."

"Or it means someone tampered with the engine."

"Where, at the beach? I looked back toward the lot a few times. Didn't see anything suspicious. Didn't see anyone, in fact."

"Could have been last night," Jill said.

"We would have had trouble before this. Wait a minute, we did have trouble, out at Vasquez."

"Not overheating. The electrical system went flooey."

"Well, I doubt if it was sabotaged," I said. "What we probably have here in this fine foreign-made vehicle is your classic lemon."

"Always the chance. Anyway, we'd better find a spot to pull over fast, or we'll conk out in the middle of the road."

We inched up the hill, the Toyota's engine losing power at an alarming rate. Now it trailed a steady stream of white smoke as the temperature gauge needle pushed deep into the red. Meanwhile the landscape darkened again, as if the creator/artist had second thoughts. The sky turned purple and the sun swelled to a wide smear of orange.

I looked up the mountain. Something dark was at the summit. At first it appeared to be a mass of dark clouds; then it transmuted into a fortress, vast and drear.

"Dracula's castle," I said.

"Huh?" Jill craned her neck and peered up. "Oh, God."

"More fun and games on Merlin's part?"

"Looks like." Jill blinked. "Hey, wait."

I looked again. It no longer looked like a castle. More like a Tibetan monastery. I began to wish that the demi-god in charge would make up his or her mind.

Jill was looking at the dashboard again. "Shit, we're going to explode."

I checked the water gauge. The needle had marched through the red warning mark and out the other side.

"Pull over as far as you can."

"Something coming up."

The road went into a hairpin turn ahead and there was enough gravel-strewn shoulder at the apex of the bend to accommodate a small car. The engine began to vibrate, then went into a series of stalls and recoveries. It finally conked out just as Jill wheeled onto the gravel and hit the brake.

She tried to restart, to no avail.

"Let's have a look," she said.

We got out, opened the hood. Jill bent over the small but complex engine, looking for all the world as though she knew what she was looking for.

"Oh, damn," she said, peering into the maze of wires, hoses, and components.

Car innards are mysterious to me. I could no more fathom them than I could the viscera of a living thing. All the analogs to living organisms are there: pumps, electrical nerve paths, lifeblood, an assortment of organs; but I have never been able to learn their workings or understand their ways.

I asked, "What's the problem?"

"Someone removed this gasket, here."

I bent closer. "Where?"

"Here, on this hose. The coolant leaked out. It was a slow leak. The sabotage could have been done last night."

"Do we have something to clamp it with?"

"No, I don't think so."

"Could the gasket have simply dropped off?"

"Not from the looks of it. Couldn't have rusted off. I think it's been tampered with."

"Might have been badly installed."

Jill shrugged. "What does it matter? There's still some coolant in the system, but not enough to make this hill.

Even if we tie it off, we'll only be able to coast back down."

We looked down the road, which to my surprise had ceased to be paved somewhere along the way. The foot of the mountain was swaddled in fog.

"No way," I said. "We're stuck."

"I guess we can't go back, at that." Jill looked at the sky. "Getting dark."

"I'd better get the computer. You want your bag?"

"Yeah. No, on second thought, to hell with it."

"Know anything about guns?"

"A little. Why?"

"Want the Remington?"

Jill shook her head. "It's your gun, you conjured it."

"That makes a difference?"

"Sure. It's your magic. Only you can make the gun work."

"You just pull the trigger."

"More to it than that," Jill said.

"If you say so."

I got the carrying bag out, checked its contents. The computer was whizzing away in full color, throwing what looked like Mandelbrot patterns, prickly leaves and involutes, infinitely regressing shorelines. It was pretty to watch.

"Oh, my God."

I looked at Jill, who stood transfixed, staring up the road. I turned.

It was a griffin, if I knew my mythical beasts. Head of an eagle, body of a lion, eagle's wings. The thing stood about eight feet tall at the shoulder—an enormous thing.

It walked down the road toward us, its four powerful legs moving smoothly in a catlike gait. It stopped about fifty feet from us and sat on its haunches, fixing us in its predator's gaze.

"Friend or foe?" I asked.

"You got me."

"What's the status of the griffin in Persian mythology?"

"I think . . . I don't really know, but I think they're good luck. Symbol of royalty."

"Would it be on our side?"

"Don't know, Skye. All I know is that it's blocking our way. We have to walk the road to get to Merlin's house."

"That's what that place is up there?"

"Must be."

"Can you be sure?"

"No, but it's a good bet."

I studied the griffin. The color of the lion part of it was more ocher than tawny, and the pelt looked like velvet. The fearsome eagle's head did not bob and twitch like a bird's head; the eyes were pitiless. No sudden movements, no fidgeting. This stately creature was not avian. The coloring of the feathers shaded from charcoal, through gray, to white. Viewed objectively, and in other circumstances, I would have thought this a magnificent if chimerical beast. We watched it spread its wings and flutter them. The beast raised its hindquarters and arched its powerful back. The sound of its wings was like the flapping of huge tents in the wind. The wings then folded and the beast resumed its former proud posture, hind cat-legs collapsed, front eagle's legs, their silver talons gleaming, extended and straight.

I had long since reached into the carrying bag to get a reassuring grip on the Remington pistol-rifle. "Should we run?" I asked.

"Where?"

I looked up the mountain. "Looks like we're trapped if it wants to do us harm."

"I don't think so," Jill said. "I'm not receiving anything evil from it. Nothing good, mind you. But nothing bad."

"It's neutral?"

"Maybe."

I kept my grip on the gun while the beast's great tail swished in the dust. The head turned. Eagle eyes regarded the still-approaching fog; then their gaze swiveled back to us.

"I hate this," I said. "I have half a mind to take a shot at it."

"How many cartridges do you have?"

"One."

"You'd better make it count."

There were several problems connected with the notion of my heroically bagging a griffin, not the least of which was the troubling fact that I had fired a gun on exactly two occasions in my entire life. I had never fired a high-powered rifle, much less a high-powered pistol-rifle. No rifle I had ever fired had ever possessed a telescopic sight, and I had no idea how such a thing would be used on a pistol. In sum, there was no reason to believe that any shot got off by yours truly would find its mark anywhere near the target, much less hit a vital spot. All the above, of course, was predicated on the assumption that the zoological phantasm in question could be killed at all.

That left running as an alternative, which was no alternative, unless we could leave the road and climb the mountain. I looked up the slopes again. Maybe, with ropes and pitons.

When I looked back the griffin had moved, turning its huge bulk around. It began to walk back up the road.

"It wants us to follow," Jill said.

"It's escorting us up to the castle?"

We looked toward the summit. The monastery was gone, replaced by a contemporary structure, a sprawling house of soaring concrete terraces and horizontal lines, hugging the edge of a cliff. The style was reminiscent of Frank Lloyd Wright in his middle period, Art Deco with a prairie flavor. The house was of the school of daring, quirky, and possibly too-faddish modern architecture for which Los Angeles has always been noted.

"That could be the real house," Jill said.

"But the real house is somewhere in Studio City, not here."

"No telling where we really are. We might have taken a magical shortcut."

"I don't think we're anywhere," I said. "This landscape strikes me as imaginary. Look at those crags, that sky. The colors. We're in an illustration. We're in one of those books you like to read."

"A fantasy world? Sure. Well, we had better start walking. Shall we?"

"I'm game."

We started off after the griffin.

19

ALTHOUGH THE GRIFFIN'S PACE WAS MODERATE, we had trouble keeping up. Twice the animal waited patiently for us, tail swishing idly, head turned to bring one golden eye around. Seeing us approach, it pointed its curving beak up the road and moved forward again.

Behind us, fog crawled up the mountain.

"We can't outrun that stuff now," Jill said, looking back. "It'll catch us in ten minutes."

"We should jog."

"Do you jog?"

"Never, but I have a feeling I'm going to regret my laziness. You?"

"I try to get out, but not every day. It's hard to find the time."

"I like that rationalization. Mind if I use it?"

"Be my guest. Do you always make jokes when you undergo stress?"

" 'Stress.' You hear that word all the time now, in all contexts. What happened to 'distress'? Or 'strain' or 'tension'?"

"They're still words, as far as I know."

"Then why is 'stress' overused? Sometimes I worry about what's happening to the language. The everyday vocabulary constantly shrinks."

"Do all English professors worry about that?"

"About shrinking vocabularies?"

"Yeah."

"What really upsets me is the daily mangling the language gets."

"So, we have to look to English professors to tell us how to speak?"

"Never! Some of them are the worst manglers."

She laughed. "You should read the stuff published in education."

"I have. A great deal of egregious nonsense comes out of that field."

Jill cast a backward glance. "What worries me is that glop. It looks like the green smoke that comes out of the sky to kill the Egyptians in *The Ten Commandments.*

"Well, let's do it."

"Jog?"

"Jog."

We jogged. For me, this was not the easiest thing to do carrying a loaded bag. The notebook computer weighed only four pounds, but the combined weight of it, the accessories, and the Remington introduced an awkward imbalance. I put my arm around the bag and held it close to my body to keep it from bouncing against me, and to bring it closer to my center of gravity. This ploy helped some.

"I don't understand one thing," I said.

"What?"

"Why I'm doing this."

"Running, or something else?"

"Ever since this started, I've wondered what's been impelling me. Why don't I listen to the warnings and catch the next plane back?"

"Curiosity?"

"I've thought about it. No. Something else."

"We'd better save our breath and not talk."

"Right."

I continued to think. I had been sucked into this mess but did not know what it was that possessed this ineluctable drawing power. Had I gone along with everything out of a sense of obligation to Grant? Hardly. Grant and I were friends but we were not close; that we moved in separate worlds was now literally true. He was dead, I was alive (for now), and there was nothing to be done about that. Why did he care about the doings of earthly computer networks? (Most of all, this question puzzled me greatly.) All right then. Was the impetus fear, fear of something horrible happening to me if I washed my hands of the affair? Perhaps, but reason told me that if I unplugged from this network of delusion and madness, I would move beyond its sphere of influence. Perhaps the anxiety experienced when I'd tried to cut loose was temporary. Had it been all that bad? Was it worse than the discomfort of uncertainty that I was experiencing now? This morning I could have demanded that Jill drive me to the airport. I had not.

On the other hand, would we have made it to the airport? Not the surest of bets. And just exactly what could I do right now to extricate myself? Not much, I had to admit. For the moment, I was stranded in a crazy dream landscape. Maybe I had no choice in the matter, had never had a choice all along. I felt something driving me. My own curiosity? It was possible. My desire to get to the bottom of this conundrum was strong, as was the need for some sort of resolution that left my sense of the universe and its cosmology intact. I needed an explanation, even one that was not the most rational of explanations.

I cast a look over my shoulder. The fog was a lot closer. Could it be moving faster now? Maybe the stuff was alive, sapient, sensing that its prey was on the verge of panic.

"Jill, look back."

She did. "God. Can you run?"

"Do we want to get ahead of the griffin?"

"Forget about the griffin, just follow the road."

Easy enough to say, but I had reservations about passing a griffin on a narrow road.

We increased our pace. I was already winded. My heart was doing strange things, bouncing around my chest cavity, flipping, flopping, maybe going into convulsions—or so I feared. I resolved to sign up at the nearest health spa the moment I got back. I made this resolution knowing full well that I would renege as soon as the danger passed.

"I hear something!" Jill shouted.

"What is it?"

"Damn it, something's chasing us again!"

I listened. Sure enough, heavy footsteps, but this time they were rapid. Again, we were being pursued, but in this exciting episode the pursuer was no dusty corpse in mummy-wrappings, no shambling hulk dragging its tentacles along. This was a creature that moved *fast*.

I looked back again. Fog hid whatever was coming.

"I can run," I said.

We broke into a long-distance pace. Both of us knew we couldn't sprint. The idea was to keep ahead, not let the thing gain on us. But even a leisurely stroll would have been taxing exertion for me. The grade had steepened and it was rough going. For me, running on the level would have been bad enough. I knew I couldn't make it, that this was the end. My nascent middle-aged body couldn't last two minutes at this pace. I would have to face whatever it was that lusted after my blood.

But I ran on.

The fog fairly raced toward us, and the pace of the footfalls that came at our heels increased greatly, almost to a gallop, if such could be said of a bipedal creature (and the sound was unmistakably that of a biped). Neither of us would make it.

"Jill, we're in trouble."

Jill kept glancing back. She was worried. When you're with a woman who is more ballsy than you, and she looks worried, that is when you know you're in deep trouble.

I began to sprint, knowing it was a desperate act. I looked up at the slopes beyond the rim of the canyon and at the rounded peaks above them, up and through which the road twined. There seemed to be a chance of our climbing to safety now. Maybe the creature couldn't climb, was too big and bulky to be an effective climber. Best not to delay making our break. If I didn't try soon, I wouldn't be in any shape to climb a stepladder.

"Let's head for the rocks!" I yelled.

Jill opened her mouth to answer but at that moment saw the same astonishing thing I did.

The griffin had stopped and, without turning, had lowered its cat-eagle body to the ground. It now reclined, sphinxlike, in the middle of the road, head erect, raptorial front feet folded under. It turned its beaked face to gather us in with one eye.

We stopped in our tracks.

"What the hell?" was all I could say.

Jill squinted her eyes, as if reading something far away. Then she looked at me. "It wants us to get on it."

"Huh?"

Jill shot forward. "Let's go!"

"But . . ."

By the time I arrived, Jill was already clambering up on the creature's back. She then crawled forward and got herself into a sitting position with her legs straddling the long feathered neck.

"Skye, get up here!"

With the beast hunkered down, the apex of the spine was only about five feet off the ground. I boosted myself up, somehow finding purchase on the short-haired, resilient pelt. I tried to be careful, chary that this fearsome imaginary critter might not take kindly to strange knees and elbows digging into its back.

"Get your arms around me!"

I straddled the backbone and slid forward until I could encircle Jill's waist with my arms. She hugged the neck.

The chimerical beast did not waste time. It rose and began to turn. I felt the hard, sharp backbone under my buttocks. Riding a vertebrate beast bareback is not the pleasantest of sensations; I had done so on a horse once or twice. This was far worse.

Completing its turn, the griffin began to run back down the road. I nearly lost my seat and flew off. The beast's back heaved under me, the spine jamming itself into some tender spots netherwards.

"Hang on!" Jill screamed.

I hugged her as hard as I could.

The beast's great wings began to flap, and this time the sound was like rolling thunder. They moved faster than any muscles could have moved them, beating the air with fantastic force. The turbulence added to the forces trying to dislodge us from our precarious seat. I slipped to one side and almost carried Jill off with me, but somehow managed to scramble back up and hold her tighter.

The beast took off. The heaving stopped and the only thing we had to deal with was the airstream and the pulsing beat of the wings. The ground dropped away. When we flew over the advancing fog front, a horrid yowl came up from below, a monstrous cry of rage and frustration. I had never heard its like, nor wanted to ever again. It sent a thousand centipedes crawling across my flesh.

The griffin began a climbing gyre, still thrashing its great pinions, gaining altitude with amazing speed. The canyon fell away, as did the slopes; then the eroded peaks of the foothills dropped far beneath us. The air grew chill, and Jill and I melded together, back to front, her dark, asymmetrically cut hair blowing in my face. It smelled like camomile.

"This is insane," I said into her ear.

"What?"

"This is insane!"

"Yeah, isn't it?"

I was reassured somehow by that reply. It was comforting to know that there was something in this world that she considered strange, out of kilter, bizarre, when judged against some notion of what was normal, meet, and proper. Jill had struck me as the sort of person who would reject standards of normality out of hand.

The improbable beast flapped higher and higher. When I began to wonder if we would pass out from lack of oxygen, the griffin leveled off, and the wings slowed and flapped only to maintain altitude. Clouds drifted by and the air turned colder. Below, the mountain range revealed itself in all its extent, and Los Angeles was nowhere in sight. We were flying over terra incognita. I could see forests, lakes, rivers, and valleys. To the right stood a high waterfall that rivaled Niagara; on the left, a lake of cerulean blue ringed by tall fir trees.

There were structures, too. Villages, hamlets, and at least two or three fair-sized towns, all with an antiquarian look to them. The exact style or period was hard to date from such a great height. Enough detail was discernible, though, to see that one or two buildings looked like temples.

Finally the wings stopped moving and stretched out to their fullest extent, and the beast began a long, smooth glide, the only sound that of the air rushing past.

I relaxed my hold on Jill. "Doesn't look much like LA down there."

"No. It's Merlin's world."

"Oh. Merlin has a world, has he?"

"You can have whatever you want on MagicNet, as long as you're good enough. Merlin's good. This is his little kingdom."

"And yonder is the castle?"

The Frank Lloyd Wright house and its grounds now occupied the high side of a range of hills. The house now took on some aspects of a castle, although the design was as one conceived in the mind of a modern architect. It missed being a masterpiece by a wide margin. Most of it was busy and overdone.

"This looks a lot like Bel Air," Jill said.

I said, "But can we be sure it's Merlin's world?"

A strange voice replied, "Of that you can be sure."
Jill looked at me. I shrugged.

"Sounded like it came from the griffin," I said.

"Did you say something?" Jill called up to the great head.

The magnificent feathered head turned slightly and the curving beak opened.

"I did. I said, you may be sure that what you see below is Kshathra, the Desired Kingdom. It is the domain of the Emperor Merlin Jones."

The beak had moved only slightly.

"Do you have a name?" Jill asked.

"My name is Asha. It means 'truth.' "

"Do you work for Merlin?"

"I work for no mortal, yet for the moment I do the emperor's bidding at the behest of the Wise Lord, Ahura Mazda."

"Oh."

I spoke into Jill's ear: "What's all that about?"

"I recognize the names from Zoroastrian mythology. That's about it."

We soared in a wide circle, tending ever downward. I could now see that the villages and towns had a vaguely Middle Eastern look to them, although I would not have characterized the style as Islamic or Arabic.

We neared the sprawling complex below, which was ringed by a network of gardens, formal and otherwise. The grounds were extensive: I spied no less than three cornfield-size swimming pools positioned among lawn tennis courts. There were at least two golf courses, one of which looked like an eighteen-holer. Palm trees and a variety of lush vegetation abounded, and nestling within all the greenery was an assortment of ponds and decorative pools. Running for miles along the ridge, a high wall, rivaling China's great one, encircled everything.

"Behold the emperor's palace," Asha said.

"A miracle of rare device," I commented.

"Indeed," Asha replied as he swooped lower.

20

MORE DETAILS OF THE COMPLEX CAME INTO VIEW: groupings of shade umbrellas, cabanas, tables, and lawn chairs. And people. They were swimming, playing tennis, lounging about, and generally disporting themselves.

As Asha banked to make his approach for a landing, I was struck by the impression that the vast majority of these vacationers were female. In fact . . .

We swooped over a network of hedgerows. When I was at the point of thinking we were going to crash, we soared over an open area, a rectangular enclosure bordered by clipped hedges, and Asha's wings began to thrash again, less vigorously this time. The powerful body shuddered as our motion slowed, and Jill and I hung on tight again. We sank, and Asha's cat-paws touched ground. No airplane ever landed like Asha, but many an avian creature had and did. He ran only a few steps after alighting.

Asha hunkered down, and we slid off his fuscous back, landing on springy, trimmed turf.

"Thank you, Asha," Jill said.

"I am glad to have been of service." Asha lifted a front leg to point toward a break in the hedgerow. "The way to the emperor's palace lies thither. I must go."

Asha retreated to the far end of the hedge-bordered courtyard. We moved to the edge. He turned, ran past us, and took off again. We watched him fly away.

When Asha was out of sight I looked around. There was in fact nothing around but grass and one low stone bench near the opposite hedge-wall.

Right then I suddenly realized that the black nylon carrying bag was still strapped over my shoulder. That I had not lost it was nothing short of miraculous. In fact, somewhere along the way I had simply forgotten about it. But here it was, still tucked under my arm. I unzipped it and checked its contents. Everything was still inside, and I was glad for that, though it seemed improbable that the gun would come in handy here. No griffin shooting had been necessary; quite the contrary, in fact.

The hedges were about eight feet tall. There was no way of getting up to peer over them; even standing on the stone bench was no help. Judging from what we had seen on landing, there was no doubt that Asha had deposited us at the center of a hedge labyrinth. The hedges themselves were too thick and brambly to allow pushing one's way through. One opening led out of the enclosure. No one was about. There seemed nothing to do but attempt to walk the maze.

"Merlin and his games," Jill said, shaking her head. "I don't fancy being chased through a labyrinth."

"Merlin has us. Why chase?"

"Let's think this through. Merlin's griffin rescues us from the bogeyman that Merlin set after us. We run to apparent safety, then *wham*, down comes the trap."

"I think at this point Merlin just wants to talk."

"To us? What about?"

We exited the central box of the maze. The choice was going right or left and we chose right.

"I think he really wants to talk to Grant," Jill said. "Make peace, somehow."

"You think Ragnarok's giving him trouble?"

"Apparently, or he wouldn't be concerned with us."

"So why doesn't he talk to Grant?"

"Best way is through your computer."

"Really? I've been getting this feeling that Grant and the computer had a parting of the ways."

"No, I don't think so. I think he's still very much a part of the architecture of that particular computer."

"I have my doubts."

"That's the way it's worked so far, but you're right that things may be changing. So I don't really know."

We turned a corner and saw that we'd chosen a blind alley. We reversed course.

"How big did this maze look to you from the air?" I asked.

"Pretty big. It might take a while to march out of it."

"Are you hungry?"

"Yup. Running always gives an appetite. Not much we can do about it."

"What time do you have?"

Jill looked at her watch. "Three-twenty."

"Is that all? Seems like ages." I glanced at mine and found that the battery had picked some time in the last few hours to run down. The digital readout was blank. "Seems as though it should be much later."

"Much later," Jill agreed.

We passed through an opening and into another corridor. We chose left this time and ran into another blind alley. Backtracking, we followed the route around a corner, found another doorway and exited through it.

After a few more turns we came to another blind alley and had to double back again. This process continued for some time as we slowly worked our way through the maze.

I stumbled and looked down. My right shoelace had come undone. Jill walked past me as I stooped to retie. The shoelace perversely chose that moment to break. I relaced as well as I could, picked up the black bag and headed for the break in the hedge through which Jill had just exited.

Passing through, I found myself in a corridor with L-corners at either hand. I had not seen in which direction Jill had walked. I moved right, turned the corner but did not see her. I called her name.

"Over here!" came her answer.

I thought that the voice had sounded from my right. I saw an opening in the hedge and turned in that direction, followed another corridor to a corner, and came up against a dead end.

"Jill! Keep talking!"

"Over here!"

I retraced my steps, or tried to, but eventually became disoriented and began to run blindly, having lost all sense of direction.

"Jill!"

No answer came. Turning feral now, I scurried like a frightened rat, half expecting to see the face of an experimenter looming in the false laboratory sky. I ran and ran.

And then, an agonizing few minutes later: "Skye?"

"Yes! Jill?"

"Skye, follow my voice."

I tried, but whichever way I turned seemed to be a bad move.

"Jill, I can't . . . Jill, where are you?"

"Right here."

I whirled, and there she was, walking toward me with an odd smile on her face. She looked pretty, damned pretty right then. I suddenly noticed how shapely her breasts were, how well constructed her body was.

"Jesus, I thought I'd lost you for good," I said breathlessly, going to her and hugging her.

She hugged back. "Sorry, Skye. Shouldn't have left you behind."

"I got a little jittery there, for a moment."

"It's okay, honey. It's okay."

She held me close, pressing her body against mine.

"I'm all right," I said. "Forget about it."

"No, it was stupid of me. Forgive?"

"Forgive. Don't worry about it."

Suddenly she tilted her head and kissed me on the mouth. I kissed back for the briefest moment, then reflexively pulled away, but she yanked me back, covering my mouth with hers. Her tongue slipped between my lips and began to probe urgently. I was astonished, appalled, and delighted, all at once, as her hands roved up and down my back and over my buttocks.

She withdrew her tongue to say, "I'm bisexual, you know. I don't usually tell people, but I am."

"Oh," I said.

"I like men sometimes. Real men."

"Oh?" I said.

"Yes."

There was something strange in her eyes, and her hand was quick, slipping down between my belly and the waistband of my sweatpants to take hold of my burgeoning manhood. Again she savagely attacked my mouth with hers, bending my head down, my neck in her crooked arm while her fingers played and stroked and measured.

Most people would not credit the notion of female rape, i.e., of a woman forcing a man to have sex. But that is exactly what happened. I was raped, which is to say that at some point in the proceedings it became abundantly clear that I was to have intercourse with this woman whether I wanted to or not. That I was willing to have intercourse with her is true but quite beside the point. I had little choice in the matter. Very soon I was on the ground with no pants and she was naked on top of me, impaling herself to the hilt; and then she bent over and began to move her slippery wetness around my anatomy as I lay there, a helpless but happy victim, my head nesting between her hanging, dark-nippled breasts.

Her thrusting was savage, primeval, and it continued well past my climax, and all the while her breath came like a furnace blast in my ear. She moaned, she whimpered, and when she brought herself to a crisis she screamed, and I was suddenly afraid, for her scream bore a faint resonance with the howl of rage I had heard when Asha swept over the advancing fog bank.

At last she was spent and lay still on me, her breathing deep and even. I dared not move, much as I wanted to get her off me and get up.

Presently she sat up, a sly, satisfied smile on her face.

"That was good. Very good. You're a good man."

"Thank you, Jill."

"My lovers call me Jahi." She passed her hand over my forehead. "Why don't you sleep now?"

"I'm really not . . . very . . ."

I opened my eyes and saw blue sky bordered by hedges. I sat up and looked around. My shoes, socks, and pants were scattered about me. The black bag was gone, and so was Jill.

I got dressed and wandered in a shell-shocked daze through the bushy labyrinth, traversing lush green corridors that led nowhere. Clueless, I must have walked for the better part of a half hour.

At long last, Jill's voice: "Skye? . . . Skye!"

I her stopped. Her again? I didn't want to see her, not just now.

Once more Jill called my name and for the second time I let her call go unanswered. A moment passed as I stood there, thinking things over.

"Skye, where are you? I found the way out."

I decided that I did not want to spend the rest of my life in this green prison, however interesting a place it was.

I called, "Here!"

"Just stay where you are!"

I sat on the manicured grass carpet and waited. A few minutes later Jill came walking through the opening a few feet away from me. She was followed by another woman, a statuesque blonde for whom the term "bombshell" must have been invented. Sun-golden, breathtakingly lovely, almost six feet tall, she wore a swimsuit that amounted to a G-string and a strip of cloth. Her hair was a golden halo and her breasts were large and cared not one whit about the law of gravity.

"There you are!" Jill said. "Sorry we lost you. It was really dumb of me to get ahead of you like that."

I rose. "Who's your friend?"

"Thought you'd like to know. Janna, may I introduce Schuyler King. 'Skye' for short."

Janna's gorgeous face split into a dazzling smile that featured pearlized teeth. "Hi, Skye!" She giggled. "Hey, that rhymes!"

"Yes, it does," I said solemnly. I was torn between gazing at Janna's spectacular body and trying to read Jill's face. Jill was acting as if nothing had happened.

"Once I got the hang of the maze, it was easy to get out," Jill told me. "Janna was at the entrance, waiting for us."

"Merlin sent me to take you back to the house," Janna said. "Are you guys ready to go now?"

Jill asked, "Skye, are you okay?"

"Fine," I said.

"Where's your bag?"

"Gone," I said.

"Gone?"

"Lost it, I guess."

"Oh." Jill looked puzzled.

"You lost your bag in here?" Janna asked. "Don't worry, we can send one of the houseboys back for it."

"Fine with me," I said. "Janna, take us to your leader."

"Sure!" Janna said brightly.

Everything Janna said, she said brightly.

21

*J*ANNA LED US OUT OF THE MAZE WITH EASE, AND
I felt stupid. Why had it seemed so vast and complex,
and how had I become so completely befuddled? The
only answer seemed to be that for all my learning and
supposed sophistication, for all those pretty diplomas
with my name in decorative calligraphy, I was feeble-
minded.

No matter. We were safe, and everything was all
right now. At least that was what my eyes, treated now
to visions that even Hugh Hefner was never vouch-
safed, were telling me. Everywhere I looked I saw wom-
en, nude or scantily clad: blondes, redheads, and all
the darker shades; Caucasian women, Oriental women,
black women, and some of indeterminate race; wom-
en volleyballing and badmintoning; women swimming,
women sunbathing, women lounging on chaises, wom-
en sipping fancy drinks as they sat under parti-colored
umbrellas, women chatting and filing their nails. Wom-
en everywhere.

This was no emperor's palace. This was a college
sophomore's wet dream, an oneiric montage of all the
centerfolds that ever stiffened the collective groin of
American manhood.

We walked past one of the swimming pools, cut across a stone terrace, and entered the main house.

"I'll take you up to Merlin's study," Janna said. "He wants to see you."

"We want to see him," Jill said, then spoke to me as we followed Janna. "It's going to be strange, meeting him in the flesh after all this time."

"How long has it been?" I asked.

"Let's see, I first met Merlin on the Net a little under two years ago. I guess it isn't so long when you think of it. Seemed like a long time."

The house was sumptuous in a showy way. We mounted a suspended stairway that curved daringly over an expansive floor. Below, more women, watching giant-screen TVs, playing table tennis, napping on the ultramodern furniture. More of this activity was transpiring in a series of spacious rooms on the second level.

The mansion was a showplace, but there wasn't much that said "home." The furniture looked fresh from the showroom, the indoor plants bore the sheen of plastic, the carpets showed no wear. The walls were splashed with garish, improbable "decorator" colors. Flashy modernist paintings hung everywhere. We walked along a gallery over an open court, in the center of which stood a giant erotic sculpture—breastoids bulging above buttocklike protrusions into which a curving phallus intruded—done in chrome. Skylights admitted the sun to nourish green coppices of vinyl and polyethylene. Everything had an artificial, ad hoc feel. I was struck by an overwhelming sense of crass, ersatz opulence, of the numbingly overdone. This was a set for a bad movie. This was self-indulgent fantasy.

Not so, however, Merlin's study.

We followed Janna through a hallway and entered an apartment that seemed to belong in another building. It looked quite lived-in and not unlike any medium-rent two-bedroom apartment in any American city. Beyond sliding glass doors at the far end of the living room, a balcony overlooked a greensward where several women in topless bikinis were playing croquet.

At a desk set against the right wall, a small, young black man sat typing at a computer terminal. There were any number of computers and their peripheral components in the room and around the apartment. Some sat on tables, some lay in various states of disassembly on the floor. Overstuffed bookshelves lined the walls, piles of books and magazines towered in the corners. To the left was a hallway with three doors, from the look of them, two bedrooms and a bath. One door was ajar, affording a glimpse of a bed, more books, computers, and clutter. The place reminded me of Grant's.

The young man, dressed in a yellow T-shirt and faded jeans, had a light complexion. I would have guessed that he had more than one white forebear. He turned his head, a half-formed impish smile playing about his lips. Baby-faced and handsome in a unique way, he was an engagingly personable young man. I guessed his age to be just short of thirty.

"Hi, Jill."

"Merlin," Jill said, "at last we meet."

"Nice to see you. You look like your computer eidolon. No nipping and tucking, no augmentation. You're an attractive woman. Unless what I'm seeing is an eidolon."

"No it isn't, and thank you very much. Speaking of attractive women . . ." Jill's eyes shifted to the view out the window.

Merlin's grin widened. "Overkill?"

"A bit. What do you do with them all?"

Merlin shrugged. "Not a whole lot. Satiety is deadening, actually. I'm hardly aware of them any more, and when I need quiet I shoo them all away. All except Janna, here."

Janna went to him and encircled her arms about his neck. "Gee, that's nice of you to say, boss."

"Can't get along without you, babe." He encircled her hips with his arm and caressed her right thigh.

Jill said, "Merlin, this is Schuyler King."

"I know. Hello, Skye, pleasure meeting you."

"Same here," I said. "I have to say that I've heard a lot about you."

Merlin chuckled. "I'm sure you did. Were you at all fair, Jill? Did you mention my good points and well as the bad?"

"I told Skye everything."

"Uh-oh. You told him about the tantrums in detail."

"Oh, you don't throw tantrums, not exactly. Sometimes you just have to have your way, and when that happens you do a great imitation of Attila the Hun."

"I insist on having my way; I confess it. The only mitigating consideration is that I know the most about the Net and how it works. I really do, Jill. Even Grant admits that."

"Merlin, shouldn't you be using the past tense when discussing Grant?"

"I'm using the present tense because Grant is present. Here. We just got done having a tête-à-tête."

Jill's dark brows rose. "Grant's here? Where?"

"In the bedroom."

"Oh?" Jill backstepped and tried to peer into the dark hallway.

"He's having a little chat with a friend of mine right now," Merlin said. "He'll be out in a minute. And then we'll all have a chat."

Jill looked at him. "I hope we can settle things, Merlin. I really do."

"I hope so too, Jill."

Janna detached herself from her boss and walked out of the room. Passing me, she touched my shoulder lightly. A strange tingling went through me.

Jill said, "Did you *have* to send a demon after Grant? Did you, Merlin?"

Jones grimaced. He looked at the floor and shook his head regretfully. "Major mistake."

"You're admitting it?"

"Oh, absolutely. Jill, you have to believe that I only wanted to scare Grant off. The demon had other ideas."

"What ideas?"

"Well, let's say that demons are subtile, in the biblical sense, but not necessarily subtle. It was after Grant's copy of Ragnarok."

I said, "That's why it trashed Grant's apartment?"

"You were there, weren't you? You saw everything."

"Heard everything. Over the phone."

"Oh. Yes, the demon was out to destroy the master Ragnarok program and all copies of it. There was no doubt that Grant had made copies, but I was pretty sure that if we acted fast enough, we could get all of them. That's the quest I charged the demon with, the task I set it to. But I didn't make my instructions explicit enough. I didn't expressly forbid it to harm Grant. I assumed that Grant would be traumatized enough by having a demon ransack his apartment. The idea was to scare the pants off him. I realize my mistake now. I simply told the demon to find the copies, destroy them, and make sure no more copies were made. Demons take the path of least resistance. The easiest way to take care of that last part was to eliminate Grant."

Jill asked, "What demon is it?"

"The Zoroastrian name is Azhi Dahaka."

"I'm not up on Persian mythology, but I'll take your word for it. Is it a particularly nasty one?"

"The nastiest, I'm afraid. And now . . ." Merlin looked off, as if scanning the house's environs with some sixth sense. "And now the son of a bitch is after me."

"Why?" I asked.

Merlin scowled. "Oh, hell, it's hard to explain. Look, why don't you guys sit down? Not much furniture around here, I'm afraid. Jill, take that director's chair. Uh, Skye . . ."

I pulled up a cardboard box with something substantial inside. "This will do."

Merlin rose, walked to the small kitchen at the front of the apartment and opened a tiny refrigerator. "Would either of you care for something to drink? I have orange juice. Let's see . . . there's beer—"

"I'd like a beer," I told him.

"Do you mind Rolling Rock? That's all I have."

"I like Rolling Rock."

"Jill?"

"Nothing for me, Merlin. Thanks."

Merlin brought me a can of beer. I snapped it open and took a drink. It went down acidly. My stomach was not in great shape. I was puzzled by the refrigerator. In the midst of the splendor of the house, why only orange juice and a few bottles of beer? Where were the servants bearing trays of fine wines and exotic liquors?

As if in answering me Merlin said, "Sorry I can't do better, but I got most of my magic committed at the moment. Takes a lot of power to ward off demons."

"Oh, I see." I nodded. Yes, stands to reason.

Merlin returned to his desk, sat, and moved a pile of printouts, revealing my laptop. Shoving his own keyboard aside, he centered the laptop in front him and studied the screen, which pulsated with color.

Merlin shook his head. "I wish I could make some sense of this. But Grant's gone beyond the final frontier. He's lost me."

"That's quite a compliment, coming from you," Jill said, sitting with long legs crossed in the shaky canvas director's chair.

"It's not a compliment. I don't think Grant is Grant."

Jill looked at me. I shrugged. Then she said, "Merlin, what do you mean?"

Merlin turned his head to say, "I don't think the entity you were talking to is Grant's spirit. I think it's someone else. Or something else."

"But you said Grant was here."

"Something that took his form. It's not Grant. I think . . . this may sound crazy. I think it's a god."

"Any particular god?" I asked.

Merlin returned his gaze to the screen. "Yes. Ahura Mazda, the Persian supreme deity."

Jill said, "I've always wondered why Persian mythology attracts you so much."

Merlin rotated in his chair and crossed his legs. "Well, I spent time in Iran in the seventies, before they booted the shah out, digging up in the mountains. Couple of sites, one an ancient Zoroastrian fire-temple and monastery."

"I know about the archaeology," Jill said. "I was talking about the attraction you have for this particular mythology."

"I was getting to that. You see, Persian mythology incorporates a lot of stuff that's central to the entire sweep of Indo-European culture. The roots are in Persia. It was a watershed that fed Indian, Euro-pagan, Judeo-Christian, and Islamic cultures. That takes in just about everything. When you work this kind of magic you're working with forces that lie at the root of the most powerful, the most efficacious culture that ever arose on this earth."

"That's an interesting attitude," I said, "considering your skin coloring."

"You have to give credit where credit is due," Merlin said. "But I didn't say 'most moral,' or 'kindest and gentlest,' did I? I didn't even say that I liked Western . . . let's call it what it is, Aryan culture. It's a dualistic culture. It gets that from the Persian influence. Black and white, good and evil, true and false. Aristotle's logic comes out of it, and all Western science."

"Fascinating."

Merlin chuckled ruefully. "I have to laugh at some of my black colleagues and their preoccupation with Islam. Man, in the slave-trading game, Arabs had a *humongous* market share. Islamic culture? You gotta be kidding me."

"How do you view what they're calling 'Afrocentrism'?"

Merlin snorted. "Are you talking about certain Egyptian fantasies, about black pharaohs building the pyramids? That's *Semitic* culture. Why they don't realize this is beyond my comprehension. Those Afrocentrist dudes are nuts. Grasping at straws. They don't know what African culture is. African culture is *totally* different from Western culture. You can't compare the two."

"No doubt," I said.

Merlin began another sentence but was brought up short by my tone, which probably rang patronizingly in his ears. Far from becoming irate, he grinned. "You're buying none of this, right? Well, look. I'm not Joseph Campbell; I don't know everything about cultures and civilizations and icons. I'm a dabbler; I dabble in everything. All I have is a robust sense of what's bullshit and what's not. And I think the Persian ethos strikes deep at the heart of things. Have you ever studied Zoroastrianism?"

I admitted that I had not.

"It's very . . . as people your age probably put it back in the sixties—it's heavy."

"I'm not quite that old."

Merlin chuckled. "Sorry."

"It's the beard. Adds a decade."

"My beard is terrible. Rather, I don't have much of one at all, and what comes up is like pubic hair."

"I've often noticed the similarity."

Merlin swung his grin to Jill. "This is one terse dude you've brought me. He doesn't talk much?"

"He's reticent. I think he still doesn't believe in MagicNet."

"You're wrong, Jill," I said. "I believe."

"He believes, Jill," Merlin intoned.

"But will I be saved or damned?"

Merlin laughed. "That, my friend, remains to be seen. Though don't mind me if I don't lift a finger to save your butt when my own posterior is in imminent danger."

"You think so?"

"I know so. You renege on a deal with a demon, and . . . well, hell, it's the oldest story in the book."

"How did you renege?" Jill asked.

"I called a truce. Dahaka doesn't care for truces. Neither does Arman, but Dahaka and Arman aren't identical. I think they're aspects of the same force, though."

Jill and I had both reacted.

Merlin looked back and forth between us. "Oh, you've met Arman, I see. He didn't tell me, though he said he was of a mind to do something about your coming here. Did he in fact do anything?"

"Just harassed us," Jill said.

"Yeah, his power in this world—I mean, the mundane world, is still shaky. He can't do much. But if Ragnarok fails, for better or worse, that will change."

"Just who the hell is this guy?" I asked.

"Arman. His real name is Ahriman. Farther back he's known as Angra Mainyu."

"What is he?"

Merlin thought about it, then said, "The devil."

"Right."

"I hear your skepticism, my friend. Okay, I can understand that. He's not the orthodox Christian devil, though. He's the Manichaean devil. Coeval with God, not created by God. Equal and opposite."

"What's his game?"

"The name of the game. That's always the question, isn't it. You can ask that of Satan—the biblical one. Why does he take his eternal stance against order? '*Non serviam!*' Why? If the deck was stacked against him, he had to know. Interesting, interesting questions, issues. Ever read any theology?"

"Not much."

"I've read spottily but earnestly, here and there. The same questions over and over, but they're worth grappling with. I've come to think the proper concern of man is simply thinking about these things. The problem of evil, for instance. Evil in the world doesn't make much sense in the Judeo-Christian scheme of things. The Jews are still wondering about the Holocaust. Why didn't skies darken? You know? What kind of God would permit it? But Zarathustra had an explanation. The world is a bad place. It's a vale of tears, right? Vale of tears. It all fits."

Merlin seemed distracted. He suddenly stopped rambling and stared out the sliding glass windows.

"What is Ragnarok?"

My question eventually pulled him back. "Hm? Oh, Ragnarok. Well, hard to say. It's an attempt to wipe out the Net and reconstruct it again. Like reformatting a hard disk."

"Is it working?"

Merlin turned to glance at the laptop. "To an extent, to an extent. But it hasn't done the job altogether. I'm still around. By the way . . ."

He reached under the desk and pulled out my black bag.

"Interesting piece, isn't it?" I said as he lifted the Remington out.

"Sure is," Merlin said, hefting it. "Beautiful, oddly beautiful." He drew a bead on the kitchen wall, sighting through the scope. "Takes some getting used to."

"I would imagine. I've never fired the thing."

"No?" He drew back the bolt and peered into the breech. Grinning, he withdrew the solitary cartridge. "Was this intended for me? I'm mortal, you know. No need for silver bullets. Or are you riffing on a completely different iconography? Like, maybe, the Lone Ranger?"

"Actually, I thought I'd be bagging a griffin or two."

Merlin chortled. "You need a scorecard."

"I realized my mistake. To tell the truth, I didn't know the score when I conjured that."

"Oh, this is a conjuring? Really." Merlin appeared surprised and delighted. "A very good one. You have natural talent."

"Thanks."

"But aren't silver bullets for werewolves?"

I lifted my shoulders. "Vampires? I'm not up on my occult lore."

"Werewolves, I think."

"The demon you sent after Grant could have passed for one."

"I thought you said you weren't actually there."

"I wasn't, but got there shortly afterward. The demon was still hanging around."

"You had a run-in with it? And you survived. Now, that is amazing in itself."

"Skye's skepticism was protecting him," Jill put in.

Merlin nodded. "I wish I didn't believe so goddamned much myself."

"Anyway," I said, "your demon did a good werewolf impression. Thus, the silver bullets."

"I'm hip."

"There's one thing I'm not hip to yet," I went on, "and I was wondering, Merlin, if you'd clear it up."

"Sure, if I can."

"What sustains MagicNet? Does it depend on computers?"

"Absolutely. Wouldn't exist without them."

"I see. There's been some speculation that that's changing. Or will change."

"Oh? Who's been speculating?"

"Grant. Me, too, actually."

"MagicNet is a computer program," Merlin said emphatically. "It would have no raison d'être if no computers existed. A computer can amplify magic.

This is fact. I ought to know. I pioneered this field."

"Did you write the original program?"

"Sure did. And many others besides."

"Grant seems to have other ideas."

"Well, that simply establishes that Grant is full of shit. You want proof? You want to know what really sustains MagicNet?"

"Sure," I said. "What is it?"

Merlin got up. "My supercomputer. It's in the other bedroom. Come on, I'll show you."

We followed him into the hallway. We passed the first bedroom door, and I cocked my ear for the sound of voices. None came. The door blocked a view of most of the room. The second bedroom door was shut. Merlin put his hand on the doorknob, then turned to us to display another version of his impish grin, this time executed with a wry twist of genuine humor.

"Prepare your minds for a new scale of physical scientific values."

If it was a joke, I didn't get it. Jill didn't laugh either. Merlin seemed not to care one way or the other. He opened the door and we stepped out of the real world again.

22

W̲E PASSED THROUGH A METAL-WALLED ANTE-
room and into a triangular tunnel that ran a short
distance. It debouched into an enormous room, at the
center of which stood a formidable machine, a polygonal
cylinder some ten feet high, studded with blinking lights
and indicators. The rest of the room followed suit. It was
a set straight out of a science fiction movie. Everything
hummed and clicked, tiny Christmas lights blinked . . .
The whole ball of wax.

Jill and I laughed.

Merlin let us have our fun, smiling tolerantly. "I like
to put on a show. But don't get the idea that it's all
show. This is a working computer. A supercomputer."

"It looks like one," I commented.

"It *is* one," Merlin said pointedly. "You have to keep
that in mind. MagicNet is running on it. It's running
all the time. And if it stops running, MagicNet ceases
to be. Got that?"

I stepped nearer the thing. It looked real enough.
Threads of gold were woven, somehow, into its trans-
lucent surface. Glints of light jumped out at the eyes.
The monstrous thing shone; it glistened.

"Now, let me get this straight," I said. "You own a
supercomputer?"

Merlin came to my side and folded his arms, admiring it with me. "No."

"Well, now, I'm confused."

"This machine is a magical construct. But it works like a supercomputer. I designed it. I'm a genuis, you see."

"I see."

It was Merlin's turn to laugh. His laugh was more of a nervous giggle. "Indulge me. Really, I love this thing. Do you understand the principle of simulating a computer with another computer?"

"Well . . . yes, I guess I understand that."

"Done all the time in computer design. That's what I did. I used magic to create the simulation. But magic makes it not a simulation, but the real thing."

"Merlin, I'm still confused. The magic that it took to create this thing—where did that come from?"

"It was small-time magic. You start small. You weave a spell. The spell creates something, and that something has the power to create something else, something bigger and better, more powerful. Can you grasp that? You build one step at a time. But it's only possible with computers. See, what I've done is, I've fused science with the occult. They're really one and the same thing. It's nothing new. Alchemy led to chemistry, astrology to astronomy. And so on, down through the ages. The ancient arts lacked rigor. So I gave them rigor."

He fell silent, and I got the impression that this explanation would have to suffice, at least for the present. I surveyed the rest of the room but somehow the detail seemed to elude me. It was a blur of flashing lights and improbable shapes, like a mental picture of something half-remembered.

"I think we should go back," Merlin finally said, and began to walk out. I followed.

"What do you think?" Jill asked me as I passed her.

"I stopped thinking forty-eight hours ago."

When we came through the tunnel, Merlin was holding the door for us. We left the antechamber, and he followed, shutting the door behind him.

Grant was seated at Merlin's desk, and Arman—this time decked out in a seersucker suit, magenta tie and vest, white shoes, pink socks, and a pink carnation—was sitting in the director's chair. He smiled pleasantly at me as I entered the living room. Janna, minus her bikini top, sat on the desk next to Grant, who was typing on the laptop's keyboard.

Merlin walked around me and peered over Grant's shoulder.

"Well?"

"Well, hell," Grant said.

Merlin snickered. "That might break loose any second."

"And well it should, for all the shit we've been pulling."

"Think we're stretching it to the breaking point?"

"I think we passed the breaking point a while back."

"How long till Dahaka breaks through my defenses?"

Grant said, "You don't have much in the way of defenses left. Most of your power is being sucked up by the system."

"Any chance of interrupting Ragnarok?"

"Ragnarok does not want to be interrupted," Grant said.

"Uh-huh."

Merlin nodded sagely, then straightened up and went to the window. He put his hands in his jeans and took a deep breath. "Shit." He shook his head. "Shit."

"Yup," Grant said. "We fucked it up royally. Even

gods can transgress the borders of the feasible."

Janna got off the desk as I approached, her perfectly shaped breasts swaying. Briefly, those breasts appeared familiar to me; but I had something else on my mind. She gave me a fetching smile, then walked around me.

I stood behind Grant. "Are you a god?"

Grant turned his head to me. "Huh?"

"Are you who you said you were, or are you someone or something else?"

Grant looked at me for a moment before returning his gaze to the ever-brightening computer screen. "Hard to say."

"I don't believe any of this is real," I said.

"Yes, you do," Arman said.

I swung around to Arman. "Then tell me who you are and why you're here."

"We're not 'here,' exactly," Arman told me. "We haven't quite returned from oblivion. We are still faint shadows, a brief parting of the mists. That is all we are, as of now. We are trying, however, to rectify the situation."

"The ancient Persian gods. Is that what all of you are?"

Arman considered the matter for a long moment. Then he said, "We are who you want us to be. If you want Persian gods, you'll get them. But I am perfectly comfortable as Ahriman. Or Satan. Or Sherlock Holmes, for that matter. Rather I should say, Professor Moriarty." A brief grin curled his purplish lips, then faded.

"Then you're some sort of chameleonlike ghost, able to assume multiple identities?"

"No, no. I am Ahriman. I am the spirit of change."

"Destruction," Grant said.

"Change. What would the universe be without it? And what is change but the disruption of old ways? Deadwood must be pruned; wreckage must be cleared away. It is creative destruction."

"Death and misery," Grant countered.

"And how would the scheme of things shape up without Death, our old friend?"

"You are Death."

"I am Death; I am many things. Let's face it, my friend, you need me. Without me the universe would be static. An impossibility."

"Without you there would be an eternal smile on the face of creation. Without you there would be joy and happiness, joy without let or hindrance everywhere."

"And complete and utter boredom." Arman yawned. "Oh, my. Excuse me. Speaking of boredom, I don't know about the breaking point, but sitting around like this is beginning to break me. I think I prefer swimming through chaos."

Grant snorted. "That doesn't get boring? Come off it."

"Are you telling me this is better?"

"To speak truth, ancient enemy of mine, the question is going to be entirely moot in but a few moments."

Merlin suddenly turned away from the window. "I still have a few ideas. Can I get in there?"

"Be my guest," Grant said, getting up. In doing so he took the Remington.

"Here, this is yours," Grant said, handing the weapon to me.

I took it. "Thanks, though I still don't know what the target is."

"You'll come to know. You created it for a specific purpose."

"But I don't know what that purpose is."

A crack of thunder sounded outside. Women screamed.

Grant took a glance at the darkening sky. "I think you'll find out very soon."

"Grant, after this is all over, are you going to tell me what it was all about?"

Grant still looked like Grant to me; he still talked like Grant and acted like him. "Skye, there are many explanations, and all of them make their own kind of sense."

"That's the problem," I said. "There are too many explanations. I only need one."

"Pick one."

I went to the sliding glass door and looked out. The sky had darkened considerably. Purple flashes began to light up the horizon. The greensward was deserted now, the women having dispersed. The trees rustled. I slid the door aside and went out. A stiff breeze rose to greet me. The landscape began to shimmer, or so I thought. I could not be sure, but it was certain that things were in a state of flux. The wind chilled me, but I stayed. I began to see things, the suggestion of a city street. Was I imagining this? I shaded my eyes. Perhaps. There was no way of telling yet. The playboy mansion bulked about me, and in the turquoise kidney-shaped swimming pool the water churned and rippled.

Bursts of color shot through the sky, and pulses of light propagated across it. Multicolored clouds swirled, grouped, and regrouped.

It grew colder. I stayed and watched until the air turned uncomfortably chill. Then I went back inside and slid the door shut.

Merlin still typed at his keyboard. At his elbow, the laptop radiated a light that was now bright enough to cause squinting. Grant was sitting on my box, reading. Arman still lounged in the director's chair, his head down. He looked asleep. I walked through the room and into the hallway.

I went to the door of the first bedroom. It was shut but not locked. I slowly pushed it open, began to walk into the room but stopped. There was a large bed against the far wall, and on it lay Janna. She saw me, and a wide inviting smile spread across her face.

"Join us," she said.

I could not move, transfixed by the sight of Jill's dark head moving between Janna's creamy thighs.

"Come here," she said, stretching out her hand. "The bed is big enough for three."

Her face and hair coloring changed in an instant, and now what confronted me was an image of Jill having sex with her twin. Then her face quickly reverted and she was the platinum centerfold bimbo again.

Jill raised her head and looked in my direction. Her eyes were glazed, and I doubt she saw me.

"Join us," Jahi commanded, for now I knew her name.

I stepped back and closed the door. It is impolitic to refuse a demon, and sometimes dangerous, but in the present circumstances I deemed my demurral a negligible risk.

I knew something else now: what I had come here to do, what I had to do.

I stepped through the door to the second bedroom.

The antechamber glowed with light spilling from the tunnel. I walked toward the light, coming out into the computer room. The machine seemed bigger now, towering above me, possessed of unknowable energy. A palpitating aureole surrounded it, stars bursting within the shimmering waves of color. The machine's yowling and whooping filled my ears—or it made no sound at all. My memory is unclear on this point. Something hurt in my head. Someone was shouting at me, hurling threats and execrations. Perhaps it was the machine itself. This monster was alive. It lived, and wanted to live longer, wanted to grow and thrive. It needed love and attention, it demanded love and attention. How dare I threaten it! How dare I deny it what it needed to live!

It wanted an answer from me. I had none. I knew only that the thing must die, that this was the central cell of the cancer, the heart of the darkness growing around me.

I raised the Remington and sighted through its mounted telescope. The cross hairs danced and shifted around the circle. I was nervous. I lowered the gun, took a deep breath, held it, then raised the gun again.

A bolt of pink lightning snaked from the machine, and I heard a loud report—and later I could not remember whether that sound was the lightning or the gun going off. Probably the latter, for the lightning or whatever it was did me no harm. The gun kicked high, and I took several steps back. I lowered the pistol-rifle and looked at the machine.

There was no appreciable damage. I thought I had missed completely. But I had not.

Cracks appeared in the machine's surface, and from these cracks a blinding light leaked and smoke streamed. The floor shook under my feet. I took a few steps back and watched the cracks widen. More smoke rose, thick, black smoke, pancaking against the ceiling while the machine gushed cascades of sparks. More electrical discharges snapped and sizzled. I smelled ozone and burning plastic. The other components of the system, the sleek shapes arrayed about the room, now began to follow suit.

A small explosion in a corner initiated a series of fires. More sparks flew, and more smoke spewed. I coughed, stepping back again, almost to the door.

The main cylinder was rending itself asunder now, revealing a heart of fire and combustion. The flames took shape, and I thought I could see a fearsome countenance in them, although for the most part its features remained indistinct. Vague eyes regarded me, angry eyes. This was no machine, but a being, whose nature I might never know. I did not want to know it. I merely wanted it to die before it did me any harm, or did the world further harm. For I knew its intentions, could discern its plans, and in those designs and schemes the puny race of man did not figure greatly, if at all.

The flames leaped but the billowing smoke obscured everything from my view. A wave of heat hit me.

The thing screamed.

The sound—or the pain inside my head—increased beyond my endurance. I dropped my weapon, its single and only round spent, and ran from the room.

As I passed through the antechamber, I heard a crash and another, very human scream, coming from the apartment. I broke into a run.

A mind-shattering sight greeted me in the living room. It is difficult for me to reconstruct it in my memory, but I will try. A giant taloned claw at the end of a long snaking arm that extended through the shattered sliding glass window. The talons gleamed, looking razor-sharp; and in their grip was Merlin, screaming hideously, crimson stains spreading on his clothing.

Slowly, agonizingly, the raptorial claw withdrew, and with it the captive and dying Merlin.

"Interesting," Grant said behind me. "Interesting."

Merlin disappeared into the maelstrom outside. I do

not know how long I stood there, looking out into the vicious cycles, the tumbling colors, the phantasmagorical light show, the enigma of it all.

"Interesting, what you did," Grant's voice said. "Never figured on that. Stroke of genius, really. I wonder who was behind it."

"I was behind it," I said, and my voice sounded strange.

Grant looked at me, and a dawning comprehension spread across his face, a face which began to fade along with the body.

"Of course. Well, you've won. Till next time. Farewell."

"Farewell," I said.

Soon, Grant was gone, Arman with him. The living room was empty.

The pain in my head came to a crescendo and here my memory becomes a complete blank.

23

THERE IS NOT MUCH MORE TO TELL.

When my memory picks up again, this is what I know—

I'm walking along a city street, a hazy blue sky above me and a fuzzy sun to my left, its golden light soft and diffuse. I pass a palm tree and stop to examine it, gazing up at its yellow-green fan of fronds. Then I move on. Before turning the corner I chance a look back and I am vaguely aware of smoke rising from a building near where the street makes a hairpin turn to climb the hill.

Then I walk down the hill and come to an intersection, rather a T, where Carpenter Avenue meets Ventura Boulevard. Across the way stands something that looks like a factory or foundry or machine shop, but which, when I cross the street and walk west along the boulevard and see its entrance, turns out to be a movie studio. I take this as a sure sign that I am in Los Angeles . . .

Again, memory fails me. I do not remember where the police picked me up, or what time of day it was. I have retained no details of my arrest and initial questioning.

There is no doubt, however, that I am in jail, and that I will be charged with at least one felony: aggravated assault. Under investigation are charges of assault with a deadly weapon, arson, and murder. They have told me that I am under suspicion of a murder committed in another state, my home state. The murder of Grant Barrington, in fact. There may be other charges, but one is minor. There is a matter of petit larceny. It is alleged that I stole a firearm, a Remington high-powered pistol, from the home of a Harlan Ellison, and it is also alleged that I used this same weapon in the commission of the aforesaid felonies. (The list of possible charges is long and includes unlawfully discharging a firearm within the confines of Los Angeles County; but this is only a misdemeanor.)

Arson? Well, they are not sure about that. However, they are sure how the fire started in Lloyd M. Jones's apartment. Someone fired a high-powered rifle bullet into a personal computer. The bullet hit the power supply, causing a short, which in turn caused a flash electrical fire that burned out three apartments on the second floor of the apartment building. The fire was the direct cause of one fatality, a Ms. Gillian Lo Bianco, an acquaintance or friend or lover of the suspect. Cause of death: smoke inhalation. She was apparently taking a nap.

There was a charge pending against Lo Bianco, stemming from a high-speed chase in which she eluded police. I have been asked how she did this. I have no answer except to say that the streets of Paris are labyrinthian, and gendarmes are easily gulled.

There was another fatality, though it may have been related to the fire only indirectly. Lloyd Merlin Jones met his death by foul play, that is clear. His body was found floating in the apartment swimming pool, which lies directly below the balcony of his apartment. However, the cause of death was not drowning. He was killed by strangulation. His body suffered multiple lacerations as well, and although he lost a great deal of blood, the lacerations were not the immediate cause of death.

No one else was hurt in the fire, and no one else was in the apartment at the time of the fire. The fire started and the murder was committed, the police think, at about the same time.

I have told them of the events of the past few days, and the police have listened patiently. I have repeated the entire story at least twice. There is one policeman, Lieutenant Mundy, who, I think, believes that I am sincere when I tell it, though I doubt he believes the story. I doubt he believes that I rode on the back of a griffin or that Merlin Jones was a wizard. They think Merlin Jones was a computer criminal, and in fact he had been under police investigation in the past. Federal authorities also have an interest in the case.

Here is what the police think. They think I was involved in computer crime, in collusion with Grant Barrington, whom I murdered because of a falling out (or because he was sleeping with one of my girlfriends, specifically Sharon—they got this from the College Green police). With another girlfriend, Gillian Lo Bianco, I flew the next day to Los Angeles to have it out with the leader of the computer theft ring, Lloyd Merlin Jones. I was going to shoot him with the gun I stole from Harlan Ellison, but there was a struggle, and the gun went off and hit one of Jones's computers. Jones and I continued to struggle, and I succeeded in strangling him, after I pushed him through the sliding window. I then threw his body over the balcony, which is how the body ended up in the swimming pool.

They found the disabled rental car in Los Flores Canyon, abandoned by the side of the road. How did Jill and I get from Los Flores Canyon all the way to Studio City, where Jones's apartment was located? We hitchhiked.

The lawyer hired by my trust officer, a Mr. Biggs, has arrived in the city. Biggs wants me examined by a court-appointed psychiatrist. He would plead me not guilty by reason of insanity. I have refused to enter this plea. Biggs continues his efforts to persuade me that I need medical attention. I am possibly schizophrenic, he says; or, possibly, I had a bad drug reaction. To what drug? He doesn't know. Perhaps, he says, I can tell him.

Excuse the police-blotter prose. I could do much better but I'm tired. I owe Biggs one debt of gratitude: he was instrumental in persuading my jailers to let me have my laptop. The police at first weren't sure that it wasn't material evidence in the case, but since the police lab examined it and found it to be an ordinary piece of computer equipment with nothing on its disk drive that could have a possible bearing on the case of *California vs. King*, they relented. With the laptop's remarkable batteries supplying power (who recharged them, I don't know—perhaps the police?), I have written this narrative with the computer's word processing software.

My cell has one window, affording a view of a tiny patch of California sky. I spend the long hours staring at it, sitting in my bunk. I am alone. I have seen one cloud in all that time. It never rains here, I am told, except sometimes in the winter. There is perpetual drought. I have read that the future holds many a rancorous battle over water rights. Yet people keep migrating to this place and the city fathers keep prodding the urban tumor to grow.

I have searched the directory of the laptop's hard disk, and as far as I can see, all of the programs that I installed on it, the programs that Grant gave me, are gone, except for one. That program is called "Restore."

Restore what? There is no way to know. I have started running the program.

Since I began running the program, the sky has changed color. At least I think so. It now has a greenish tinge, and there are, I believe, faint streaks of yellow in it. But I am only seeing a very small portion of sky. Perhaps other things are happening in other parts of the sky. Or not. It could be a trick of light.

After finishing this narrative, there will not be much for me to do but stare through the bars, out the window. But if something is going to happen I want to see it happening. So I will wrap this up, and then I will sit and watch the sky.

DeChancie, JOhn
   MagicNet
(1)

DATE DUE

AUG 2 3 2000			
AUG 3 1 2000			
SEP 1 3 2000			

SOMERSET COUNTY LIBRARY

6022 Glades Pike

Somerset, PA 15501

(814) 445-5907

10 cents per day overdue fines